11-13-00

HarperPerennial
A Division of HarperCollins*Publishers*

Dogs Are Worth It!

PEANUTS TREASURY

Charles M. Schulz

HarperCollins books may be purchased for educational, business, or sales promotional use.
For information please write to:
Special Markets Department, HarperCollins Publishers, Inc.,
10 East 53rd Street, New York, NY 10022

http://www.harpercollins.com

Designed by Christina Bliss, Staten Island

ISBN 0-06-107563-9

Printed in U.S.A.

HI, CHUCK..JUST CALLING TO WISH YOU A HAPPY NEW YEAR...
DO YOU LOVE ME, CHUCK?
1-1-93
I'M SORRY, BUT YOUR CALL CANNOT GO THROUGH..PLEASE HANG UP, AND DO NOT DIAL AGAIN..
© 1992 United Feature Syndicate, Inc.
SCHULZ

I'M THINKING MAYBE WHEN I GROW UP, I'LL BE A BEAUTY QUEEN..
1-2-93
© 1992 United Feature Syndicate, Inc.
DO YOU HAVE TO BE REALLY BEAUTIFUL?
PROBABLY
DO THEY HAVE A SORT OF FAIRLY, KIND OF, YOU KNOW, CUTE QUEEN?
SCHULZ

PEANUTS®
by SCHULZ
KING OF THE HILL!

I AM THE KING! I AM THE KING OF THE HILL!
1-3-'93
I AM THE QUEEN! I AM THE QUEEN OF THE HILL!!
I AM THE ATTORNEY! I AM KING OF THE HILL! I HAVE THE DEED OF TRUST!
SCHULZ

"Will you miss me while I'm gone?" he asked.
"Why?" she said. "Where are you going?"
"Don't you remember?" he said. "I'm going on an expedition, and I'll be gone for twenty-five years."
1-4-93
© 1992 United Feature Syndicate, Inc.
"I'm sorry," she said. "I guess I wasn't listening."
SCHULZ

YES, MA'AM.. I BROUGHT MY DOG TO SCHOOL TODAY.. WELL, SOMETIMES HE GETS LONELY...
1-5-93
© 1992 United Feature Syndicate, Inc.
NO, MA'AM.. HE WON'T CREATE A DISTURBANCE..
SCHULZ
MAYBE..
Z

MA'AM? MY DOG WANTS TO GO OUT IN THE HALL FOR A DRINK OF WATER..
1-6-93
© 1992 United Feature Syndicate, Inc.
A LITTLE PROBLEM, MA'AM.. THERE'S A FOUNTAIN OUT THERE, BUT NO WATER DISH.. DO YOU HAVE A WATER DISH?
DOGS ARE WORTH IT, MA'AM..
SCHULZ

A TRUE OR FALSE TEST? YES, MA'AM
DO YOU MIND IF MY DOG TAKES THE TEST, TOO? YOU KNOW, JUST FOR THE FUN OF IT...
1-7-93
© 1992 United Feature Syndicate, Inc.
IT'LL GIVE HIM SOMETHING TO DO
HOW DO YOU MAKE "T'S" AND "F'S"?
SCHULZ

TRUE..FALSE..
TRUE..FALSE..
TRUE..TRUE..
FALSE..TRUE..
© 1992 United Feature Syndicate, Inc.
HOW ARE YOU DOING?
1-8-93
SCHULZ
NO PEEKING!

HERE'S MY TEST PAPER, MA'AM..
AND HERE'S MY DOG'S TEST PAPER..
WE NEVER HAD "TRUE OR FALSE" TESTS AT OBEDIENCE SCHOOL
© 1992 United Feature Syndicate, Inc.
THEY WERE CALLED "SIT OR ELSE"
SCHULZ
1-9-93

HE DID WHAT?
SHE SAYS YOU GOT THE ONLY PERFECT SCORE ON THE "TRUE OR FALSE" TEST!
© 1993 United Feature Syndicate, Inc.
1/11
NO, MA'AM, I DON'T KNOW HOW HE DID IT..
WHAT'S TRUE IS TRUE, AND WHAT'S FALSE IS FALSE..
SCHULZ

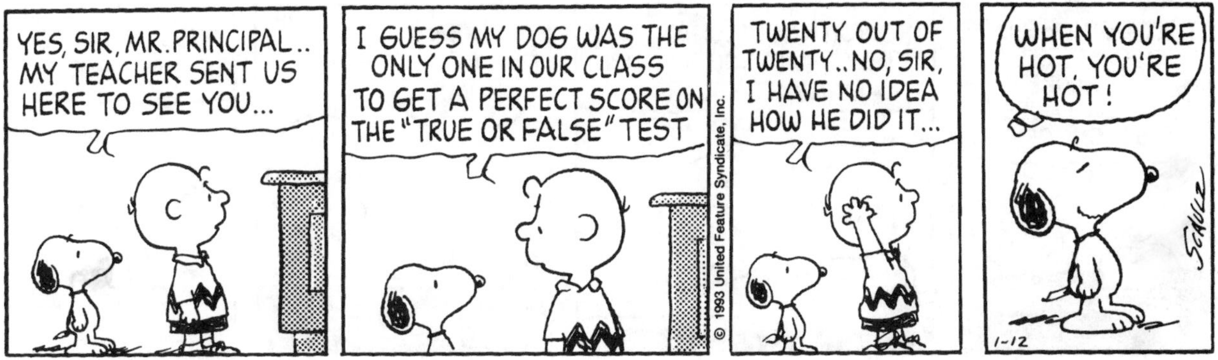
YES, SIR, MR. PRINCIPAL.. MY TEACHER SENT US HERE TO SEE YOU...
I GUESS MY DOG WAS THE ONLY ONE IN OUR CLASS TO GET A PERFECT SCORE ON THE "TRUE OR FALSE" TEST
© 1993 United Feature Syndicate, Inc.
TWENTY OUT OF TWENTY..NO, SIR, I HAVE NO IDEA HOW HE DID IT...
WHEN YOU'RE HOT, YOU'RE HOT!
1-12
SCHULZ

NO, SIR.. I DIDN'T HELP HIM.. I DIDN'T KNOW SOME OF THE ANSWERS MYSELF..
1-13
YES, SIR.. HE GOT A PERFECT SCORE... NO, HE DIDN'T CHEAT..
© 1993 United Feature Syndicate, Inc.
SCHULZ
NO, SIR, WE'RE NOT MAKING FUN OF YOUR SCHOOL..

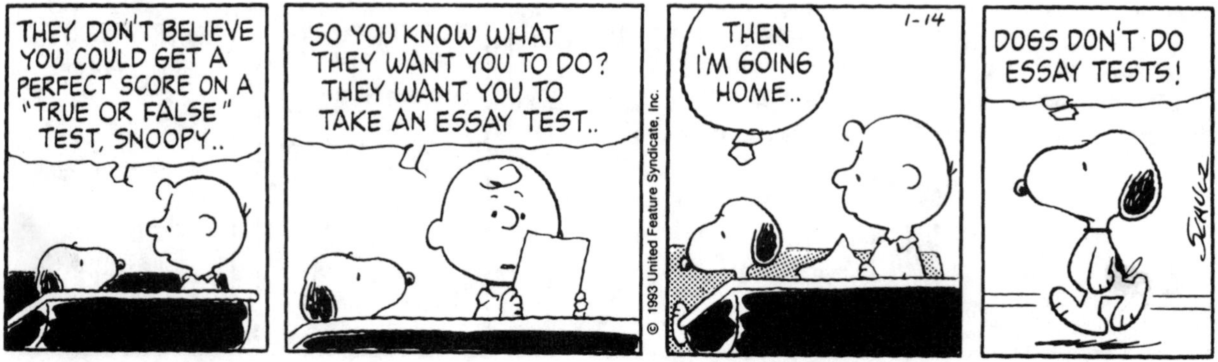
THEY DON'T BELIEVE YOU COULD GET A PERFECT SCORE ON A "TRUE OR FALSE" TEST, SNOOPY..
SO YOU KNOW WHAT THEY WANT YOU TO DO? THEY WANT YOU TO TAKE AN ESSAY TEST..
© 1993 United Feature Syndicate, Inc.
1-14
THEN I'M GOING HOME..
DOGS DON'T DO ESSAY TESTS!
SCHULZ

NO, MA'AM..MY DOG DIDN'T COME TO SCHOOL TODAY..
NO, I STILL DON'T KNOW HOW HE GOT A PERFECT SCORE ON THE "TRUE OR FALSE" TEST
1-15
© 1993 United Feature Syndicate, Inc.
MAYBE IT'LL ALWAYS BE A MYSTERY...
I NEVER CAN REMEMBER..DID THE "T" STAND FOR "TRUE" OR FOR "FALSE"?
SCHULZ

I THINK I'M GETTING SMARTER EVERY DAY..
GOOD FOR YOU
© 1993 United Feature Syndicate, Inc.
DID YOU KNOW THERE'S NO SCHOOL ON SATURDAYS? I WENT DOWN THERE TODAY, AND ALL THE DOORS WERE LOCKED..
1-16
I FIGURED THAT ONE OUT IN A HURRY!
SCHULZ

MARTIN LUTHER KING SAID, "I HAVE A DREAM"
BEFORE THAT, WE WOULDN'T BE SITTING HERE..
AND I WOULDN'T BE TRADING YOU A CARROT STICK FOR A FRENCH FRY..
THAT'S NOT AN EVEN TRADE, FRANKLIN..
© 1993 United Feature Syndicate, Inc.
1-18
SCHULZ

I'VE BEEN WORRIED ABOUT YOU..HOW ARE YOU STANDING THE COLD WEATHER?
© 1993 United Feature Syndicate, Inc.
1-19
SCHULZ

© 1993 United Feature Syndicate, Inc.
TELL THE BUS TO HURRY UP.. I'M FREEZING TO DEATH!
WHERE'S YOUR BROTHER?
I THINK I'M IN HERE SOMEPLACE..
SCHULZ
1-20

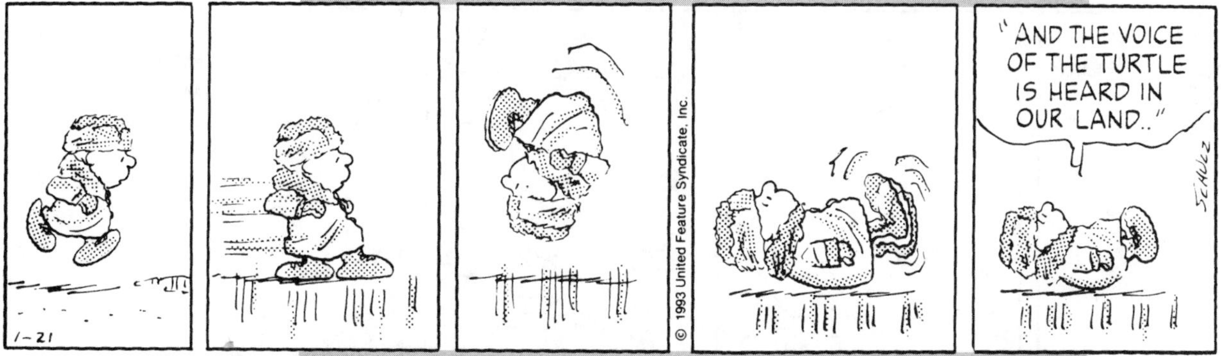
1-21
© 1993 United Feature Syndicate, Inc.
"AND THE VOICE OF THE TURTLE IS HEARD IN OUR LAND.."
SCHULZ

THIS IS RIDICULOUS! I'M LIKE A TURTLE.. I CAN'T GET UP!
I COULD LIE HERE ALL WINTER..
MAYBE SOMEONE WILL COME ALONG, AND HELP ME..
DO YOU MIND IF I PLAY THROUGH?
© 1993 United Feature Syndicate, Inc.
1-22
SCHULZ

WHY ARE YOU LYING HERE ON YOUR BACK LIKE A TURTLE, BIG BROTHER?
I SLIPPED ON THE ICE, AND NOW I CAN'T GET UP..
I'M GOING TO HAVE TO LIE HERE FOR THE REST OF MY LIFE..
SHOULD I START MOVING MY THINGS INTO YOUR ROOM?
© 1993 United Feature Syndicate, Inc.
1-23
SCHULZ

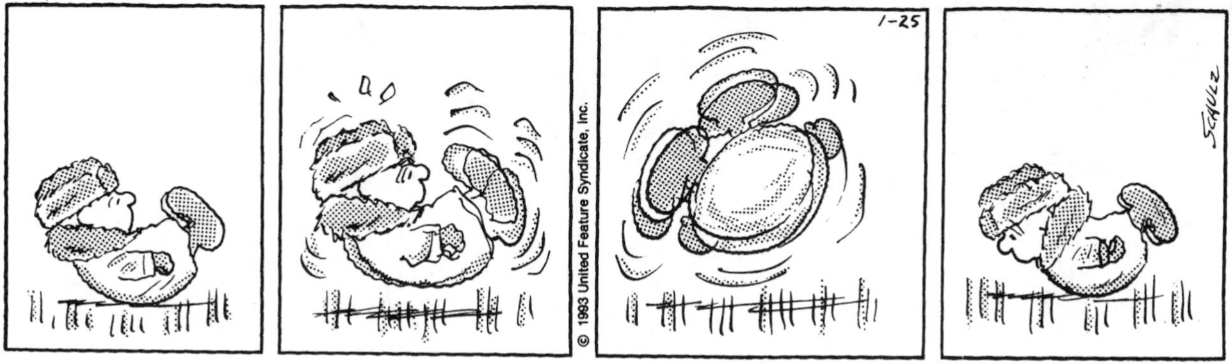
1-25
SCHULZ

SNOOPY! YOU'VE COME TO RESCUE ME! YOU CAN PUSH ME ALL THE WAY HOME..
KEEP PUSHING, BUT BE CAREFUL WHEN WE GET TO THE..
1-26
..CURB!
SCHULZ

HERE'S THE WORLD FAMOUS HOCKEY PLAYER ON HIS WAY TO THE GAME..
1-27
UNDER THE NEW RULES IF YOU START A FIGHT, YOU ARE AUTOMATICALLY EJECTED FROM THE GAME...
© 1993 United Feature Syndicate, Inc.
SO I MIGHT AS WELL GO HOME NOW..
SCHULZ

Dear Brother Snoopy, Guess what! It snowed here last night!
I didn't know it snowed in the desert.
1-28
I guess we learn something new every day, don't we?
© 1993 United Feature Syndicate, Inc.
WHOP!
Like, I didn't know coyotes could throw.
SCHULZ

1-30
MY GRAMPA SAYS HE TAKES ONE HUNDRED AND FOUR STROKES WITH HIS RAZOR WHEN HE SHAVES..
© 1993 United Feature Syndicate, Inc.
HE COUNTED THEM?
GRAMPA IS RETIRED.. HE DOESN'T HAVE MUCH ELSE TO DO..
SCHULZ

NO, I DIDN'T SEE A POLAR BEAR RUN BY HERE..
DOES HE KNOW YOU'RE CHASING HIM?
© 1993 United Feature Syndicate, Inc.
YES, THAT'S PROBABLY WHAT HAPPENED..
HE WAS RUNNING SO FAST I DIDN'T SEE HIM..
2-2
SCHULZ

PEANUTS®
by
SCHULZ

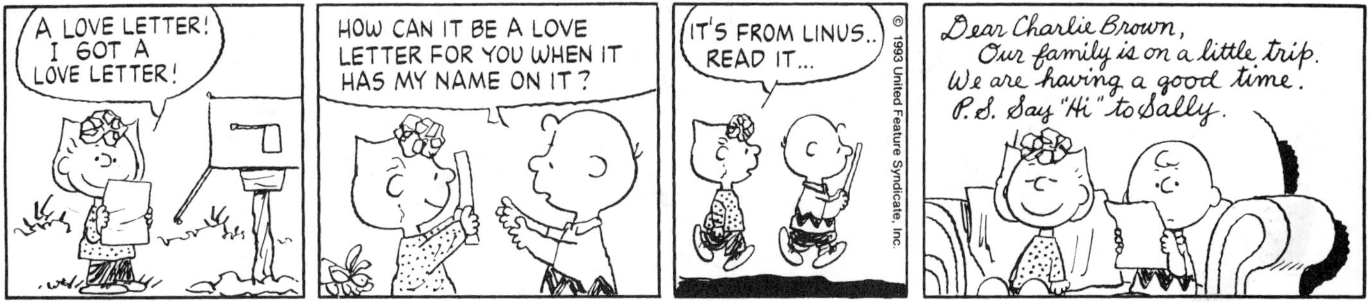
A LOVE LETTER! I GOT A LOVE LETTER!
HOW CAN IT BE A LOVE LETTER FOR YOU WHEN IT HAS MY NAME ON IT?
IT'S FROM LINUS.. READ IT...
© 1993 United Feature Syndicate, Inc.
Dear Charlie Brown,
Our family is on a little trip.
We are having a good time.
P.S. Say "Hi" to Sally.

SEE? HE SAID, "SAY 'HI' TO SALLY"... IF THAT ISN'T A LOVE LETTER, I DON'T KNOW WHAT IS!
1-24
I THINK I'LL PASTE IT IN MY SCRAPBOOK..
MY FIRST LOVE LETTER!
HOW ROMANTIC..
SCHULZ

DIDN'T CATCH THE POLAR BEAR, HUH?
2-3
© 1993 United Feature Syndicate, Inc.
WHAT ARE YOU GOING TO DO NOW?
NO, I DON'T KNOW WHAT A MOOSE TASTES LIKE..
SCHULZ

WHAT HAPPENS IF YOU CAN'T SPEAR A POLAR BEAR OR A MOOSE?
2-4
© 1993 United Feature Syndicate, Inc.
SCHULZ
YOU SPEAR THE WILD CHOCOLATE CHIP COOKIE!

SEE, MARCIE? MY AD IS IN THE PAPER..
" HELP WANTED.. ATTRACTIVE YOUNG LADY CAN'T REMEMBER HISTORY DATES"
"DOESN'T UNDERSTAND FRACTIONS.. CALL PATRICIA REICHARDT AT NUMBER BELOW.."
2-5
WHAT DO YOU THINK, MARCIE?
YOU ARE EXTREMELY WEIRD, SIR
© 1993 United Feature Syndicate, Inc.
SCHULZ

SOMETIMES I LIE AWAKE AT NIGHT, AND I ASK, "IS IT ALL WORTH IT?"
THEN A VOICE SAYS, "WHO ARE YOU TALKING TO?"
© 1993 United Feature Syndicate, Inc.
THEN ANOTHER VOICE SAYS, "YOU MEAN, 'TO WHOM ARE YOU TALKING?'"
NO WONDER I LIE AWAKE AT NIGHT!
2-6
SCHULZ

I HAVE A NEW PHILOSOPHY.. "LIFE IS LIKE A GOLF COURSE"
AND "A SAND TRAP RUNS THROUGH IT"
2-8
© 1993 United Feature Syndicate, Inc.
SCHULZ

STANDING IN THE RAIN WAITING FOR THE SCHOOL BUS SHOWS A DESIRE FOR AN EDUCATION THAT LEADS TO COLLEGE AND A JOB WITH A BIG SAN FRANCISCO LAW FIRM..
HERE, HIT HIM WITH A LUNCH BOX!
2-9
SCHULZ
© 1993 United Feature Syndicate, Inc.

YES, MA'AM..MY HEAD SORT OF HURTS...I THINK MAYBE I HAVE THE GOLLYWOPPERS...
2-10
© 1993 United Feature Syndicate, Inc.
YES, MA'AM..I HAD A FLU SHOT ABOUT A MONTH AGO..
NO, MA'AM..THE AVERAGE FLU SHOT HAS NO EFFECT ON THE GOLLYWOPPERS..
SCHULZ

HOW DID EVERYTHING GO AT SCHOOL TODAY, MARCIE? REMEMBER? I HAD TO GO HOME
2-11
© 1993 United Feature Syndicate, Inc.
SOMEBODY BROKE INTO THE CUSTODIAN'S CAR, THE DRINKING FOUNTAIN FELL OFF THE WALL, AND THAT STUPID KID IN THE BACK ROW ATE THE LAST PIECE OF CHALK...
RATS! I ALWAYS MISS THE GOOD DAYS!
SCHULZ

SURE, LIFE IN THE DESERT CAN BE LONELY AT TIMES..
2-12
BUT AT LEAST YOU KNOW YOU'RE NOT GOING TO GET HIT IN THE FACE WITH A PIE...
© 1993 United Feature Syndicate, Inc.
PROBABLY..
SCHULZ

"I DON'T KNOW," SAID THE FARMER.."I'M NOT A COW!"
2-13
© 1993 United Feature Syndicate, Inc.
HA HAHAHAHA
ROCKS NEVER LAUGH AT ANYTHING..
SCHULZ

THAT LITTLE RED HAIRED GIRL IS AT THE DOOR...
SHE SAYS SHE FORGOT TO GIVE YOU A VALENTINE SO SHE CAME BY TO GIVE IT TO YOU NOW...
APRIL FOOL!!
..OR FEBRUARY OR MARCH OR WHATEVER
2-15
SCHULZ
© 1993 United Feature Syndicate, Inc.

DOES YOUR SISTER EVER AGGRAVATE YOU?
HOW MANY HOURS ARE IN THE DAY?
WHAT WAS THE QUESTION?
WHO ARE THEY TALKING ABOUT?
DID SOMEBODY MENTION COOKIES?
2-16
SCHULZ
© 1993 United Feature Syndicate, Inc.

LINUS, DO ME A FAVOR... ASK THAT LITTLE RED-HAIRED GIRL IF SHE EVER GOT THE VALENTINE I SENT HER...
2-17
HEY!
© 1993 United Feature Syndicate, Inc.
SAY, KID..THE TEACHER WANTS TO KNOW WHY YOU'RE CRAWLING OUT THE DOOR..
SCHULZ

I'LL BE THE SHEPHERD AND YOU BE A SHEEP, OKAY?
2-18
© 1993 United Feature Syndicate, Inc.
YOU'RE SUPPOSED TO SAY, "BAA!"
SCHULZ

ROCK
SLIDE
AREA

WE SHEPHERDS HAVE A FAVORITE SAYING..
© 1993 United Feature Syndicate, Inc.
" GOD TEMPERS THE WIND TO THE SHORN LAMB "
WHATEVER THAT MEANS
2-19
SCHULZ

HERE'S THE LONELY SHEPHERD STANDING OUT UNDER THE STARS..
ALL HIS SHEEP HAVE GONE ASTRAY... IT'S SO SAD..
© 1993 United Feature Syndicate, Inc.
YOU'RE NOT CRYING..
SCHULZ
2-20

DON'T EVEN THINK IT!
© 1993 United Feature Syndicate, Inc.
IF I CAN'T SAY IT, I HAVE TO THINK IT..
SCHULZ
2-22

© 1993 United Feature Syndicate, Inc.
IN
OUT
SCHULZ
2-23

WELL, I IMAGINE THE REASON YOU CAN'T THROW A SNOWBALL IS YOU DON'T HAVE ANY HANDS..
OF COURSE, YOU COULD ALWAYS JUST "WING" IT!
© 1993 United Feature Syndicate, Inc.
HA HA HA HA HA
2-24
SCHULZ

I'M NOT GOING TO SCHOOL TODAY, MARCIE.. I HAVE A COLD...
SHALL I BRING SOME OF YOUR SCHOOL WORK HOME SO YOU CAN DO IT TONIGHT?
2-25
© 1993 United Feature Syndicate, Inc.
ARE YOU OUT OF YOUR MIND?
SCHULZ
I DON'T UNDERSTAND SICK PEOPLE..

NO, MA'AM, PATRICIA ISN'T HERE TODAY... SHE HAS A COLD..
NO, MA'AM, SHE DOESN'T WANT ME TO TAKE HER HOMEWORK TO HER..
2-26
© 1993 United Feature Syndicate, Inc.
ARE YOU OUT OF YOUR MIND?
JUST QUOTING HER, MA'AM..
SCHULZ

© 1993 United Feature Syndicate, Inc.
2-27
SCHULZ

3-1
HERE'S MY EXCUSE, MA'AM, FOR MISSING SCHOOL LAST WEEK..
DON'T TRY TO STAND IT UP...IT'S A PRETTY LAME EXCUSE
© 1993 United Feature Syndicate, Inc.
HAHAHAHA
THANK YOU, MA'AM.. I'M GLAD I'M BACK, TOO..
SCHULZ

3-2
© 1993 United Feature Syndicate, Inc.
YOU'RE THE ONLY ONE I KNOW WHO CAN LAND WITH BACKSPIN..
SCHULZ

"THE FLOW OF WIND OVER THE TOP OF THE KITE MOVES FASTER THAN THE AIR BEHIND THE KITE'S LEADING EDGE CREATING A VACUUM WHICH CAUSES LIFT.."
3-3 © 1993 United Feature Syndicate, Inc.
SCHULZ

FOR "SHOW AND TELL" THIS MORNING I HAVE A TURTLE WHICH I SAVED WHEN IT WAS TRYING TO CROSS THE ROAD..
IT ISN'T ?
FOR "SHOW AND TELL" THIS MORNING I HAVE A HUBCAP WHICH I SAVED WHEN IT WAS TRYING TO CROSS THE ROAD..
© 1993 United Feature Syndicate, Inc.
3-4
SCHULZ

MY GRAMPA SAYS THAT AFTER ALL THESE YEARS, HE STILL DOESN'T UNDERSTAND LIFE
© 1993 United Feature Syndicate, Inc.
FOR INSTANCE, LAST WEEK HE BOUGHT A NEW CAR..
3-5
BUT HE GOT THE FLU ANYWAY..
SCHULZ

3-8
AH CHOO
© 1993 United Feature Syndicate, Inc.
BLESS YOU
SCHULZ

PEANUTS®
by SCHULZ

THE DOCTOR IS IN

PSYCHIATRIC HELP 5¢
THE DOCTOR IS IN
?!
3-7
THE DOC IS IN
THE DOCT IS IN
YOU'RE A BLOCKHEAD! FIVE CENTS, PLEASE..
SCHULZ

THIS BUTTER IS PRACTICALLY FROZEN..
NOBODY TOLD ME LIFE WAS GOING TO BE THIS HARD!
I HATE GETTING UP IN THE MORNING.. SCHOOL DRIVES ME CRAZY...
..AND NOW I HAVE TO BUTTER MY TOAST WITH CHUNKY BUTTER!
"CHUNKY" BUTTER?
© 1993 United Feature Syndicate, Inc.
3/9
SCHULZ

THIS IS A NICE LIBRARY, MA'AM..
I NEED A COUPLE OF BOOKS...DO YOU HAVE "A TALE OF TWO TOWNS" BY CHARLES WHAT'S-HIS-NAME?
3-10
© 1993 United Feature Syndicate, Inc.
YOU HAVE IT! THIS IS GREAT..
NOW HOW ABOUT "THE BROTHERS SOMETHING OR OTHER"?
SCHULZ

IS THE SCHOOL BUS HERE YET?
YOU DON'T SEE IT, DO YOU?
MY, AREN'T WE CRABBY TODAY..
I'M NOT CRABBY.. I FEEL FINE..
3-11
© 1993 United Feature Syndicate, Inc.
GOOD..MAY I ASK YOU A PERSONAL QUESTION?
SURE, GO RIGHT AHEAD..
IS THE SCHOOL BUS HERE YET?
SCHULZ

YOU'RE ALWAYS SAYING BEETHOVEN WAS SO GREAT...
DID BEETHOVEN EVER SERVE ON A SUB-COMMITTEE? HUH? DID HE?
© 1993 United Feature Syndicate, Inc.
3-12
KLUNK!
HOW CAN YOU BE CALLED GREAT IF YOU'VE NEVER SERVED ON A SUB-COMMITTEE?
SCHULZ

It was a dark and stormy night.
3-13
© 1993 United Feature Syndicate, Inc.
HOW CAN YOU BE SO SURE?
If I remember correctly, it was a dark and stormy night.
SCHULZ

DON'T TELL ME YOU'RE GOING TO TRY PLAYING BASEBALL AGAIN..
I HAVE TO.. IT'S MY DESTINY...
WHEN SPRING COMES, I'M DRAWN TO THE BALL FIELD! I FORGET EVERYTHING ELSE..
3-15
© 1993 United Feature Syndicate, Inc.
DON'T FORGET TO FEED THE DOG..
SCHULZ

I CAN'T PLAY TODAY, MANAGER.. I COULDN'T FIND MY GLOVE..
WOULDN'T IT BE FUNNY IF IT TURNED OUT THAT YOUR GLOVE WAS ON YOUR HEAD AND YOUR CAP ON TOP OF YOUR GLOVE?
I'LL GO HOME AND LOOK AROUND AGAIN..IF I CAN'T FIND IT, JUST START WITHOUT ME..
© 1993 United Feature Syndicate, Inc.
3-16
SCHULZ

NOW, WHEN WE ASK HIM IF YOU CAN PLAY, DON'T LET HIM KNOW YOU'RE SO SHORT
YOU HAVE A FRIEND WHO WANTS TO PLAY ON OUR TEAM?
WHERE?
© 1993 United Feature Syndicate, Inc.
3-17
SCHULZ

HOW COULD HE PLAY ON OUR TEAM? HE'S TOO SHORT!
© 1993 United Feature Syndicate, Inc.
3-18
SNIF!
WELL, ASK HIM IF MAYBE HE'D LIKE TO BE OUR BAT BIRD..
SCHULZ

HOW ARE THINGS IN LEFT FIELD, PIGPEN?
I PUT BURNT CORK UNDER MY EYES JUST LIKE THE PROS..
© 1993 United Feature Syndicate, Inc.
"PAINTING THE LILY," HUH?
PAINTING THE WHAT?
SCHULZ
MANAGERS ARE ALWAYS SAYING STRANGE THINGS..
3-19

ALL RIGHT, EVERYONE OVER HERE FOR THE TEAM PHOTO!
YOU HAVE YOUR CHOICE.. YOU CAN SIT WITH EITHER PIGPEN OR THE DOG...
WHAT KIND OF A CHOICE IS THAT?
I SHOULD THINK IT WOULD BE OBVIOUS
I'LL TAKE TEN 5X7, TWELVE 8X10, AND TWENTY WALLET SIZE..
SCHULZ
3-20
© 1993 United Feature Syndicate, Inc.

I HEARD THE COYOTES HOWLING AGAIN LAST NIGHT, CHARLIE BROWN..
I WONDER IF IT'S AN OMEN THAT WE'RE GOING TO LOSE THE FIRST GAME OF THE SEASON...
© 1993 United Feature Syndicate, Inc.
THAT'S RIDICULOUS! WE'RE GOING TO WIN! I DON'T BELIEVE IN OMENS..
3-22
BUT THEY SOUNDED SO EERIE..
MAYBE IT WAS AN OMEN THAT WE'RE GOING TO LOSE THE SECOND GAME OF THE SEASON..
SCHULZ

I CAN'T BELIEVE IT..
3-23
OUR BASEBALL SEASON STARTS TODAY, AND WE HAVEN'T LOST YET..
© 1993 United Feature Syndicate, Inc.
OF COURSE, I HAVEN'T GOTTEN OUT OF BED YET, EITHER..
SCHULZ

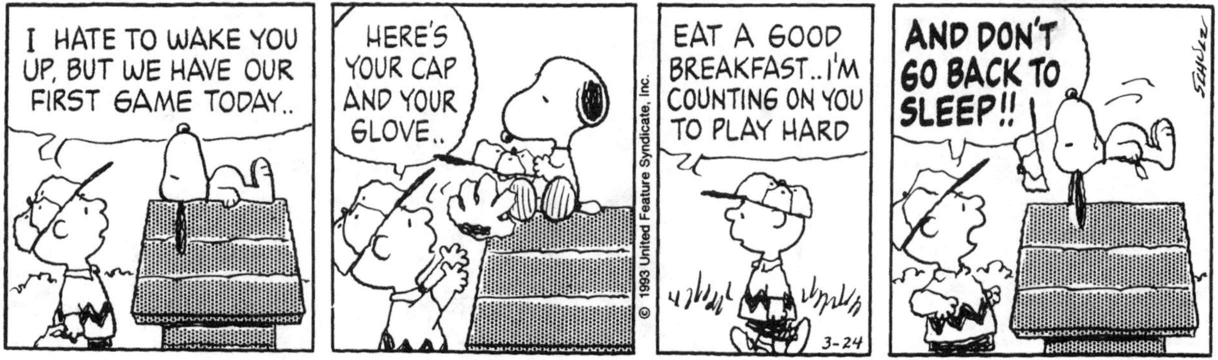
I HATE TO WAKE YOU UP, BUT WE HAVE OUR FIRST GAME TODAY..
HERE'S YOUR CAP AND YOUR GLOVE..
© 1993 United Feature Syndicate, Inc.
EAT A GOOD BREAKFAST.. I'M COUNTING ON YOU TO PLAY HARD
3-24
AND DON'T GO BACK TO SLEEP!!
SCHULZ

I FEEL UP FOR THE GAME TODAY! I REALLY THINK WE CAN WIN!
I FEEL GOOD MENTALLY, AND I FEEL GOOD PHYSICALLY.. THIS IS THE MOST CONFIDENT I'VE EVER FELT...
3-25
© 1993 United Feature Syndicate, Inc.
YOU'VE GOT GRAPE JELLY ON YOUR SHIRT..
SCHULZ

ONE FINGER WILL MEAN YOUR FAST BALL WHICH ISN'T VERY FAST ANYWAY..
TWO FINGERS WILL BE YOUR CURVE WHICH DOESN'T CURVE AT ALL..
THREE FINGERS WILL BE YOUR CHANGE-UP WHICH HASN'T FOOLED ANYONE YET...
FOUR FINGERS WAS FOR A PITCH-OUT, BUT WE WON'T USE THAT ONE
WHY NOT?
3-26
© 1993 United Feature Syndicate, Inc.
EVERYTHING YOU THROW LOOKS LIKE A PITCH-OUT!
SCHULZ

3-27
HELLO? OH, HI! HOW ARE YOU?
OH, NOTHING.. JUST PLAYING IN THIS STUPID BALL GAME..YEAH, RIGHT FIELD..
© 1993 United Feature Syndicate, Inc.
SHE DID? SHE WORE THE PINK ONE AGAIN? I CAN'T BELIEVE IT! SHE...
BONK!
SORRY.. WE WERE CUT OFF..
SCHULZ

THIS IS IT, CHARLIE BROWN..LAST INNING.. TWO OUTS... AND YOU'RE UP!
ALL THE PRESSURE IS ON ME, BUT I CAN DO IT! I KNOW I CAN DO IT...
3-29
JUST DON'T GET NERVOUS..
© 1993 United Feature Syndicate, Inc.
HERE, YOU'D BETTER USE A BAT..
SCHULZ

I HIT A HOME RUN IN THE NINTH INNING, AND WE WON! I WAS THE HERO!!
YOU?!
SCHULZ
3-30
© 1993 United Feature Syndicate, Inc.

THE BALL CAME RIGHT OVER THE PLATE..
3-31
THEN, POW! YOU HIT IT OVER THE FENCE, AND WE WON THE GAME!
© 1993 United Feature Syndicate, Inc.
THEIR PITCHER WAS IN TOTAL SHOCK..
YEAH, I CAN STILL SEE THE LOOK ON HER FACE!
SCHULZ

ARE YOU THE KID WHO HIT THE HOME RUN OFF ME YESTERDAY?
WELL, I HOPE YOU'RE SATISFIED! YOU RUINED MY WHOLE LIFE!
YOU CAME CLEAR OVER HERE TO TELL ME THAT?
NO, I WAS JUST KIND OF CURIOUS TO SEE WHERE YOU LIVE..YOU PROBABLY HAVE A DOG, TOO, DON'T YOU?
SORT OF..
WHAT DO YOU MEAN, SORT OF?
4-1
© 1993 United Feature Syndicate, Inc.
SCHULZ

HEY, KID! WAIT A MINUTE! I DON'T KNOW YOUR NAME!
ROY HOBBS WAS MY GREAT-GRANDFATHER..WHEN YOU HIT THAT HOME RUN YESTERDAY, YOU RUINED MY LIFE!
I JUST MET THE GREAT-GRANDDAUGHTER OF ROY HOBBS!
I NEVER KNOW WHAT YOU'RE TALKING ABOUT..
4-2
© 1993 United Feature Syndicate, Inc.
SCHULZ

WHERE'S THE SUGAR?
MOM PUT IT IN THE REFRIGERATOR TO KEEP IT AWAY FROM THE ANTS..
© 1993 United Feature Syndicate, Inc.
SCHULZ
4-3
JUST WHAT I NEED... COLD SUGAR..

4-6
"THINGS FALL APART; THE CENTER CANNOT HOLD"
© 1993 United Feature Syndicate, Inc.
WHEN CATCHERS GET HIT WITH TOO MANY FOUL BALLS, THEY GET A LITTLE WEIRD..
SCHULZ

PEANUTS®
by SCHULZ

4-4
© 1993 United Feature Syndicate, Inc.
SCHULZ

YOU LEAD A BORING LIFE, DID YOU KNOW THAT? YOU NEVER DO ANYTHING EXCITING
BLEAH!!
THAT WAS EXCITING..
© 1993 United Feature Syndicate, Inc.
SCHULZ
4-7

4-8
HOW ABOUT SHARING YOUR UMBRELLA?
© 1993 United Feature Syndicate, Inc.
SCHULZ

IT'S HARD TO BE A SHEPHERD WITHOUT ANY SHEEP..
4-9
OF COURSE, THERE WAS LITTLE BO-PEEP WHO HAD SOME SHEEP, BUT THEN SHE LOST THEM
© 1993 United Feature Syndicate, Inc.
BUT MAYBE IT'S BETTER TO HAVE LOST YOUR SHEEP THAN NEVER TO HAVE HAD ANY SHEEP AT ALL..
I THINK I'M CRACKING UP
SCHULZ

4-10
YOU SHOULD WRITE A SELF-HELP BOOK..
YOU KNOW, TO HELP THOSE WHO ARE LONELY AND CAN'T GO ANYPLACE..
© 1993 United Feature Syndicate, Inc.
How to be Happy Even Though You're Stuck in the Back Yard.
SCHULZ

WHO WON THE "SPLENDID BOWL" THIS YEAR, SIR?
"SUPER BOWL," MARCIE
4-12
WHATEVER.. WAS IT A GOOD GAME?
YOU'RE NOT MUCH FOR SPORTS, ARE YOU, MARCIE?
© 1993 United Feature Syndicate, Inc.
I GUESS NOT..BUT SOMETIMES I GET A LITTLE CURIOUS...
DID ANYBODY MAKE A HOLE-IN-ONE?
SCHULZ

THIS IS MY REPORT ON RAIN
TO KEEP FROM GETTING WET, IT IS BEST TO CARRY AN UMBRELLA SIMILAR TO THIS ONE...
4-13
© 1993 United Feature Syndicate, Inc.
YES, MA'AM, I HAVE SEVERAL MORE PROPS..A PAIR OF BOOTS, THREE SANDBAGS AND VARIOUS PHOTOGRAPHS OF CLOGGED STORM DRAINS...
OKAY, LET'S FORGET THE PROPS..
SCHULZ

I SEE IT'S RAINING AGAIN, MA'AM.. MY DOG IS GOING TO GET WET...
4-14
YES, MA'AM.. HE HAS A DOGHOUSE, BUT HE CAN'T GO IN IT BECAUSE HE HAS CLAUSTROPHOBIA..
© 1993 United Feature Syndicate, Inc.
I COULD GO IN THERE... I KNOW I COULD.. ALL I'D HAVE TO DO IS DO IT.. I COULD JUST DO IT...
I THINK I'M GETTING WET..
SCHULZ

YOU'RE A BLOCKHEAD AND AN AIRHEAD!
YOU'RE A NOODLENECK!
4-15
YOU'RE A PUZZLEWIT AND A DIMBULB!
© 1993 United Feature Syndicate, Inc.
THE OLD WORDS STILL WORK THE BEST..
SCHULZ

DID ANYONE CALL WHILE I WAS OUT?
I DIDN'T KNOW YOU WERE OUT
WELL, DID ANYONE CALL?
CALL WHO?
ME! DID ANYONE CALL ME WHILE I WAS OUT?
WHY WOULD ANYONE CALL YOU?
AS SOON AS I'M THIRTY-FIVE, I THINK I'LL LEAVE HOME..
SCHULZ
4-16

4-17
I WONDER WHAT IT WOULD BE LIKE IF OUR ROLES WERE REVERSED..
WHAT IF YOU WERE THE MASTER AND I WERE YOUR DOG?
I THOUGHT I WAS THE MASTER..
SCHULZ

DID YOU FALL IN LOVE THE FIRST TIME YOU SAW ME ?
NO, YOU DIDN'T IMPRESS ME THAT MUCH
HOW ABOUT NOW? HOW DO YOU FEEL NOW WHEN YOU LOOK AT ME ?
WELL, WHEN I TWIST AROUND LIKE THIS, IT SORT OF HURTS MY NECK..
HOLD STILL.. I'M GOING TO HIT YOU WITH MY NOTEBOOK
© 1993 United Feature Syndicate, Inc.
4-19
SCHULZ

WHERE'S THE STUPID SCHOOL BUS ?
I DON'T THINK IT'S COMING..
HOW LONG ARE WE SUPPOSED TO WAIT ?
TWO MORE HOURS AND I'LL BE IN HIGH SCHOOL..
I'D GO BACK HOME, BUT MY MOM AND DAD HAVE PROBABLY MOVED AWAY
U.S. MAIL
© 1993 United Feature Syndicate, Inc.
4-20
SCHULZ

4-21
© 1993 United Feature Syndicate, Inc.
I DON'T THINK THE SCHOOL BUS IS EVER GOING TO COME..
I THINK THEY'VE FORGOTTEN ABOUT US..
MAYBE WE SHOULD START WALKING..
DOES ANYONE REMEMBER THE NAME OF OUR SCHOOL?
SCHULZ

I HAVEN'T WALKED TO SCHOOL IN A LONG TIME
GRAMPA SAYS HE ALWAYS WALKED TO SCHOOL..
FIVE MILES! IN ZERO WEATHER!
IN DEEP SNOW!
UPHILL!
4-22 © 1993 United Feature Syndicate, Inc.
SCHULZ

WHO'S THIS GUY?
THE PRINCIPAL.. WE HAVE TO TELL HIM WHY WE'RE LATE
TELL HIM THE BUS DIDN'T COME, AND WE WALKED ALL THE WAY
ASK HIM IF HE REMEMBERS ANY OF US..
4-23
SCHULZ
© 1993 United Feature Syndicate, Inc.

SOMETIMES I LIE AWAKE AT NIGHT, AND I ASK, "WHY AM I HERE?"
THEN A VOICE SAYS, "WHERE ARE YOU?"
© 1993 United Feature Syndicate, Inc.
"HERE," I SAY... "WHERE IS 'HERE'?" SAYS THE VOICE..
"WAVE YOUR HAND SO I CAN SEE YOU"
THE NIGHTS ARE GETTING LONGER..
SCHULZ
4-24

JOE GRUNGE
4-26
© 1993 United Feature Syndicate, Inc.

4-27
TIRED OF PUSHING ALREADY?
© 1993 United Feature Syndicate, Inc.

SCHULZ
4-28
© 1993 United Feature Syndicate, Inc.

HOW DOES THIS SOUND, MARCIE? "AND THE PROPHET SAID THEY WOULD BEAT THEIR SWORDS INTO GOLF CLUBS"
"PLOWSHARES"
4-29
© 1993 United Feature Syndicate, Inc.
TRY PLAYING EIGHTEEN HOLES WITH A PLOWSHARE, MARCIE! HA HA HA HA!!
YOU ARE EXTREMELY WEIRD, SIR..
SCHULZ

THIS NEXT GUY IS THEIR BEST HITTER..EVERY TIME HE'S UP, HE HITS A HOME RUN...
WHAT SHOULD I DO?
HOLD ON TO THE BALL UNTIL HE GOES AWAY
© 1993 United Feature Syndicate, Inc.
4-30
SCHULZ

5-1
FROM A DISTANCE, A BIRDBATH AND A SUNDIAL LOOK A LOT ALIKE..
© 1993 United Feature Syndicate, Inc.
SCHULZ

GRAMPA SAYS HE WENT TO SCHOOL FOR TWELVE YEARS, AND WAS NEVER ALLOWED TO DRAW ON THE BLACKBOARD
HE SAYS HE WAS DEPRIVED OF ONE OF THE GREAT JOYS OF LIFE..
HE SAYS SOME NIGHT AFTER A PTA MEETING, HE'S GOING TO DRAW ALL OVER ONE OF THE BLACKBOARDS..
CAN HE DRAW PRETTY WELL?
NO, ALL HE EVER DRAWS IS MICKEY MOUSE..
© 1993 United Feature Syndicate, Inc.
SCHULZ
5-3

I'M NOT GOING TO SCHOOL ANYMORE BECAUSE I ALREADY KNOW EVERYTHING I'LL EVER NEED TO KNOW..
HOW FAR AWAY IS THE MOON, WHEN WAS GEORGE WASHINGTON BORN AND WHAT'S THE FRENCH WORD FOR TOOTHPASTE?
I HOPE I HAVE A CUPCAKE IN MY LUNCH TODAY..
© 1993 United Feature Syndicate, Inc.
SCHULZ
5-4

WHAT ARE YOU WATCHING?
I DON'T KNOW
I MEAN, I KNOW WHAT I'M WATCHING, BUT I DON'T KNOW WHAT'S GOING ON
WELL, ACTUALLY, I KNOW WHAT'S GOING ON, BUT I'VE SORT OF LOST TRACK..
WHY IS BARNEY PURPLE?
5-5
SCHULZ
© 1993 United Feature Syndicate, Inc.

I'VE GOT THE NUMBERS FIGURED OUT, BUT WHO ARE THESE PEOPLE WITH THE FUNNY CLOTHES, AND WHAT GAME ARE WE PLAYING, ANYWAY?
COOKIES
I'VE GOT THE NUMBERS FIGURED OUT, BUT WHO ARE THESE PEOPLE WITH THE FUNNY CLOTHES, AND WHAT GAME ARE WE PLAYING, ANYWAY?
5-6
SCHULZ
© 1993 United Feature Syndicate, Inc.

5-7
© 1993 United Feature Syndicate, Inc.
FIRST-TIME CARD PLAYERS, SNOOPY AND RERUN, QUICKLY DISCOVER THAT THE GAME IS MORE FUN WHEN PLAYED WITH A DOUBLE DECK!
SCHULZ

TAKE A LETTER..
5-8
© 1993 United Feature Syndicate, Inc.
I'VE ALWAYS WANTED TO SAY THAT..
SCHULZ

WOODSTOCK! CONRAD! BILL! RAYMOND! FRED! ARE WE ALL HERE?
JUST OUT OF CURIOUSITY, HOW COME NONE OF YOU HAS A BIRD NAME?
?
NO, YOU'RE RIGHT...I WOULDN'T WANT TO BE CALLED "TWEETIE"
5-10
© 1993 United Feature Syndicate, Inc.
SCHULZ

WHERE'S YOUR STUPID DOG?
HE'S TAKING HIS TROOPS ON ANOTHER NATURE HIKE
HA! HE'LL BE LUCKY IF HE EVER FINDS HIS WAY HOME!
5-11
© 1993 United Feature Syndicate, Inc.
..AND, I HATE TO ADMIT IT, BUT IF YOU'RE LOST, THE BEST WAY TO FIND YOUR WAY HOME IS TO FOLLOW A CAT..CATS ALWAYS KNOW WHERE THEY'RE GOING..
SCHULZ

RIGHT UP AHEAD YOU'RE GOING TO SEE THE FAMOUS "BALANCING ROCK"
"BALANCING ROCK" HAS BEEN PERCHED ON THIS CLIFF FOR TEN MILLION YEARS, AND...
5-12
© 1993 United Feature Syndicate, Inc.
I GUESS WE SHOULD HAVE COME YESTERDAY..
SCHULZ

HERE'S A REAL TREAT FOR ALL OF US... A CHANCE TO DRINK PURE WATER FROM A COOL MOUNTAIN STREAM..
© 1993 United Feature Syndicate, Inc.
NO, FRED.. I DIDN'T BRING ANY STRAWS!
5-13
SCHULZ

I HAVE A SURPRISE FOR YOU..
BEFORE WE ALL GO TO SLEEP, I'M GOING TO READ A LITTLE FROM MY FAMOUS NOVEL, "IT WAS A DARK AND STORMY NIGHT"
Z
Z
Z
Z
Z
5-14
© 1993 United Feature Syndicate, Inc.
SCHULZ

YOUR STUPID DOG DIDN'T COME HOME LAST NIGHT
NO, I GUESS HE'S CAMPING OUT WITH HIS TROOPS..
GATHER 'ROUND, MEN, AND WATCH ME FLIP THESE PANCAKES!
SORRY, CONRAD
5-15
© 1993 United Feature Syndicate, Inc.
SCHULZ

WELL, I SEE YOU'RE BACK FROM YOUR CAMPING TRIP..
I HOPE YOU ENJOYED IT AS MUCH AS THE BIRDS..
© 1993 United Feature Syndicate, Inc.
I DON'T KNOW..I HATE CHIRPING AROUND THE CAMPFIRE..
SCHULZ
5-17

LEND ME YOUR PEN, WILL YOU, MARCIE?
5-18
THEN LET ME HAVE YOUR PENCIL..
© 1993 United Feature Syndicate, Inc.
TIME OUT, MA'AM, FOR AN EQUIPMENT CHANGE!
SCHULZ

Z

PEANUTS
by SCHULZ
SHOW HIM HOW, BIG BROTHER!
BRUSH HIM BACK!

STRIKE HIM OUT, BIG BROTHER! YOU CAN DO IT! STRIKE HIM OUT!!
© 1993 United Feature Syndicate, Inc.

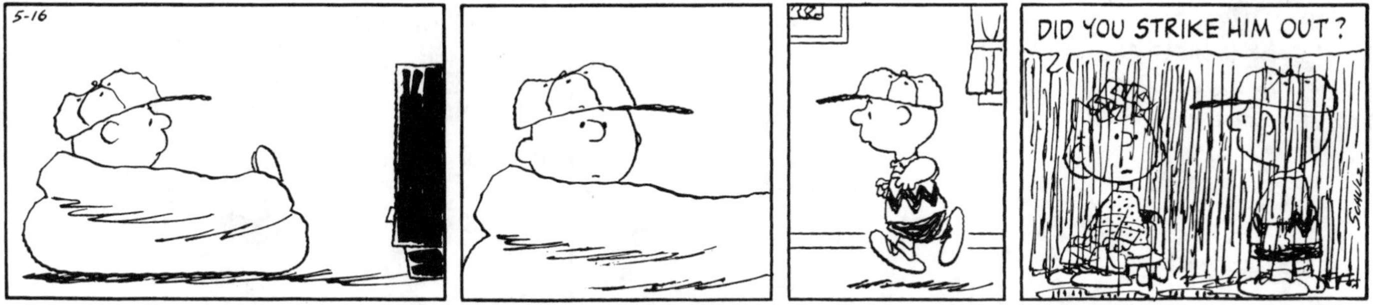
5-16
DID YOU STRIKE HIM OUT?

5-19
AS A WORLD FAMOUS ATTORNEY, WOULD YOU EVER BE INTERESTED IN BECOMING A MEMBER OF THE SUPREME COURT?
WHY NOT?
© 1993 United Feature Syndicate, Inc.
OF COURSE, YOU'D HAVE TO MOVE TO WASHINGTON..
WHERE'S THAT?
SCHULZ

Dear Mr. President,
Apparently there is soon to be an opening on the Supreme Court.
© 1993 United Feature Syndicate, Inc.
I would like to recommend a friend of mine who is a world famous attorney.
WHERE SHOULD I TELL HIM YOU WENT TO LAW SCHOOL?
YOU'D BETTER SKIP THAT PART..
SCHULZ
5-20

© 1993 United Feature Syndicate, Inc.
5-21
I CAN SEE YOU NOW SITTING ON THE BENCH OF THE SUPREME COURT.. THEY'D PROBABLY PUT YOU RIGHT NEXT TO JUDGE SANDRA DAY O'CONNOR..
IS SHE CUTE?
SCHULZ

A JUDGE ON THE SUPREME COURT?! THAT STUPID DOG COULDN'T BE A JUDGE ON A TENNIS COURT!
AU CONTRAIRE! HE IS AN ATTORNEY WITH THE HIGHEST OF REPUTATIONS!
WHAT HAPPENED TO ALL THE COOKIES?
SCHULZ
5-22
© 1993 United Feature Syndicate, Inc.

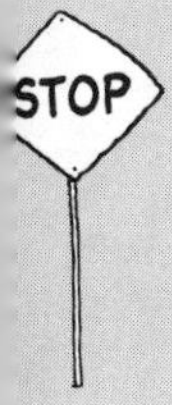
STOP

OKAY, LET'S SAY THE PRESIDENT HAS APPOINTED YOU TO THE SUPREME COURT...
© 1993 United Feature Syndicate, Inc.
NOW, YOU'RE FACING THE SENATE JUDICIARY COMMITTEE, AND SENATOR BIDEN ASKS YOU A TOUGH QUESTION.. HOW WILL YOU RESPOND?
WOOF!
5-24
I THINK YOU'RE IN!
SCHULZ

HERE'S THE WORLD FAMOUS ATTORNEY ON HIS WAY TO WASHINGTON TO TAKE HIS SEAT ON THE SUPREME COURT..
WHAT'S THIS? A FUNNY LOOKING DOG DRESSED UP LIKE AN ATTORNEY!
© 1993 United Feature Syndicate, Inc.
5-25
WHAP!
"THE LAW IS EVERMORE THE LEADER IN SOCIETY"
SCHULZ

YOUR STUPID DOG JUST LEFT FOR WASHINGTON
HE WHAT?
LINUS TALKED HIM INTO TRYING OUT FOR THE SUPREME COURT
SNOOPY! COME BACK!
© 1993 United Feature Syndicate, Inc.
HERE'S THE WORLD FAMOUS ATTORNEY ON HIS WAY TO WASHINGTON TO TAKE HIS SEAT ON THE SUPREME COURT..
I DIDN'T EVEN GET TO THE JUDICIARY COMMITTEE..
5-26
SCHULZ

HOW COULD YOU THINK THEY'D EVER LET YOU BE A JUDGE ON THE SUPREME COURT?
YOU CAN'T EVEN DECIDE IF YOU'LL HAVE YOUR SUPPER IN THE RED DISH OR THE YELLOW DISH..
5-27
© 1993 United Feature Syndicate, Inc.
OR YOUR DRINKING WATER IN THE GREEN DISH OR THE BLUE DISH!
THOSE DISHES SHOULD ALL BE THE SAME COLOR..
SCHULZ

5-28
ONE FINGER WILL MEAN A FAST BALL, TWO FINGERS A CURVE, AND THREE FINGERS WILL MEAN TURN AROUND AND TRY TO HIT YOUR RIGHT-FIELDER IN THE HEAD WITH THE BALL!
GAME CALLED ON ACCOUNT OF DARKNESS! WHERE'D EVERYBODY GO? I CAN'T SEE A THING!
© 1993 United Feature Syndicate, Inc.
SCHULZ

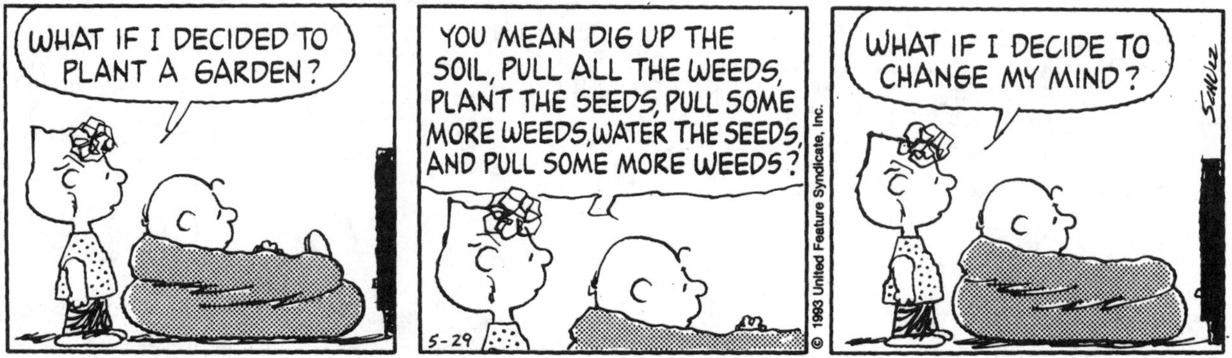
WHAT IF I DECIDED TO PLANT A GARDEN?
YOU MEAN DIG UP THE SOIL, PULL ALL THE WEEDS, PLANT THE SEEDS, PULL SOME MORE WEEDS, WATER THE SEEDS, AND PULL SOME MORE WEEDS?
5-29
© 1993 United Feature Syndicate, Inc.
WHAT IF I DECIDE TO CHANGE MY MIND?
SCHULZ

WHEN YOU DIE, ARE YOU EVER ALLOWED TO COME BACK?
ONLY IF YOU HAD YOUR HAND STAMPED..
5-31
© 1993 United Feature Syndicate, Inc.
SCHULZ

SLEEP WELL, OL' PAL..TOMORROW WILL BE A NEW DAY, AND WE NEVER KNOW WHAT EXCITEMENT LIES AHEAD..
ACTUALLY, I CAN'T TELL ONE DAY FROM THE OTHER..
© 1993 United Feature Syndicate, Inc.
SCHULZ

HOW ABOUT THIS, MARCIE? IT LOOKS LIKE SHE GAVE ME AN "A" IN EVERY SUBJECT...
6-3
© 1993 United Feature Syndicate, Inc.
YOU'RE RIGHT.. HER "D-MINUSES" DO LOOK LIKE "A'S"
SCHULZ

YOU KNOW WHAT I THINK, CHUCK? I THINK YOU GET BETTER GRADES IF YOU'RE CUTE..
I'LL BET MY TEACHER WOULD HAVE GIVEN ME ALL "A'S" IF I LOOKED LIKE THIS..
6-4
© 1993 United Feature Syndicate, Inc.
I LIKED YOU FINE THE OTHER WAY..
THANK YOU, CHUCK
BOY, THAT HURTS YOUR EYES..
SCHULZ

I SUPPOSE A LONG-DISTANCE RUNNER LIKE YOURSELF WATCHES WHAT HE EATS..
6-5
ABSOLUTELY
© 1993 United Feature Syndicate, Inc.
AFTER I'M DONE, I ALWAYS EAT A POWER DOUGHNUT..
SCHULZ

MY GRAMPA SAYS THOSE WERE THE GOOD DAYS..
6-7
WHAT DAYS ?
© 1993 United Feature Syndicate, Inc.
HE DOESN'T KNOW WHAT DAYS, BUT HE'S SURE THOSE WERE THE GOOD DAYS..
SCHULZ

© 1993 United Feature Syndicate, Inc.
6-8
THAT WAS FUN!
STUPID DOG!
SCHULZ

I'LL JUST SIT HERE, AND LET YOU DIVIDE THE COOKIES BETWEEN US..
DOGS CAN'T COUNT
SCHULZ
© 1993 United Feature Syndicate, Inc.
6-9

I'M SORRY I'M LATE WITH YOUR SUPPER.. I STOPPED TO ADMIRE THE SUNSET..
THERE WAS A GLOW IN THE SKY LIKE I'VE NEVER SEEN BEFORE..
6-10
© 1993 United Feature Syndicate, Inc.
I DON'T THINK THERE'S A WORD THAT DESCRIBES HOW IT CAN MAKE YOU FEEL...
HUNGRY!
SCHULZ

SO HERE I AM RIDING ON THE BACK OF MY MOM'S BICYCLE..
THIS SHOULD BE A GOOD TRIP IF SHE STEERS STRAIGHT...
© 1993 United Feature Syndicate, Inc.
..AND IF OUR FRONT WHEEL DOESN'T GO DOWN THAT..
6-11
..GRATE!
SCHULZ

ALL RIGHT, TROOPS..BEFORE YOU GO TO SLEEP, I WANT TO HEAR SOME BEDTIME PRAYERS..
I DIDN'T KNOW THEY HAD THEOLOGICAL DIFFERENCES..
6-12
SCHULZ
© 1993 United Feature Syndicate, Inc.

SOMETIMES, CHUCK, I WONDER IF YOU EVER REALIZE JUST HOW EMBARRASSING THIS CAN BE..
6-14
SCHULZ
© 1993 United Feature Syndicate, Inc.

IT'S A BEAUTIFUL SIGHT, ISN'T IT?
?
WHAT DO YOU MEAN, DID I USED TO COME HERE WHEN I WAS YOUNG?! I'M NOT THAT OLD!
6-15
© 1993 United Feature Syndicate, Inc.
?
NO, I NEVER KNEW BILLY THE KID!
SCHULZ

WHEN I WENT INTO TOWN TO PLAY GOLF, THEY ASKED ME WHAT MY HANDICAP IS...
6-16
I SAID MY HANDICAP IS I'M A DOG..
THEN THEY SAID DOGS AREN'T ALLOWED ON THE COURSE..
© 1993 United Feature Syndicate, Inc.
SO I THOUGHT MAYBE I'D SUE..
BUT DOGS AREN'T ALLOWED IN THE COURTHOUSE..
SCHULZ

BONK
6-17
LUCY, YOU'RE THE WORST PLAYER IN THE HISTORY OF THE GAME!
YOU CAN'T PROVE THAT! YOU SHOULD NEVER SAY THINGS THAT YOU CAN'T PROVE!
IN ALL PROBABILITY, YOU ARE THE WORST PLAYER IN THE HISTORY OF THE GAME!
© 1993 United Feature Syndicate, Inc.
I CAN ACCEPT THAT..
SCHULZ

DID YOU KNOW THAT BLACKBEARD, THE PIRATE, BURIED ALL HIS GOLD HERE IN THE DESERT?
6-18
AND THAT BLACKBEARD ONCE SPENT THE NIGHT IN A MOTEL IN NEEDLES? THAT'S WHAT SOMEONE TOLD ME..
© 1993 United Feature Syndicate, Inc.
YOU DON'T BELIEVE ANYTHING, DO YOU?
SCHULZ

HEY, KID.. REMEMBER ME? I'M ROY HOBBS' GREAT-GRANDDAUGHTER
I KNOW.. I'M VERY IMPRESSED
THE LAST TIME WE PLAYED, YOU HIT A HOME RUN OFF ME, AND RUINED MY LIFE!
6-21
© 1993 United Feature Syndicate, Inc.
I WAS JUST LUCKY
I SUPPOSE YOU THINK YOU'RE GONNA DO IT AGAIN..
WHAT'RE YOU TRYIN' TO DO NEXT, RUIN MY AFTERLIFE?
SCHULZ

YOU'RE UP NEXT, CHARLIE BROWN.. YOU CAN HIT THIS PITCHER! THE LAST TIME YOU FACED HER, YOU HIT A HOME RUN!
6-22
© 1993 United Feature Syndicate, Inc.
YOU CAN DO IT! YOU'RE THE HERO TYPE!
OR THE GOAT TYPE..
SCHULZ

6-23
THAT ROUND-HEADED KID IS UP NEXT, ISN'T HE?
SO WHAT? HE WAS JUST LUCKY THE LAST TIME WE PLAYED...
© 1993 United Feature Syndicate, Inc.
YOU'RE ROY HOBBS' GREAT-GRANDDAUGHTER, AREN'T YOU? WELL, SHOW 'IM WHO YOU ARE!
THROW IT IN HERE, ROYANNE!
ROYANNE?
SCHULZ

6-24
STRIKE ONE!
© 1993 United Feature Syndicate, Inc.
C'MON, CHARLIE BROWN! SHE'S NO PITCHER! SHE'S ONLY A GIRL!
ONLY A GIRL?!
WELL, I'M ONLY YOUR SISTER, YOU BLOCKHEAD!!
SCHULZ

HEY, I THOUGHT I FELT A DROP OF RAIN..
6-25
I DID! IT'S RAINING!
STRIKE TWO!
© 1993 United Feature Syndicate, Inc.
HA! YOU'RE DOOMED, KID! YOU'RE GONNA STRIKE OUT!!
NO, I'M GONNA DROWN..

© 1993 United Feature Syndicate, Inc.
TWO STRIKES ON THAT ROUND-HEADED KID, AND IT STARTS RAINING!
MAYBE IT'LL STOP SOON..
YOU CAN GET A HIT, CHARLIE BROWN..DON'T LET THAT GIRL STRIKE YOU OUT!
SHE THROWS PRETTY HARD..
I'M A HOUSE DOG.. HOUSE DOGS AREN'T SUPPOSED TO GET WET
6-26

OKAY, KID, IT'S STOPPED RAINING, AND YOU GOT TWO STRIKES AGAINST YOU!
TIME OUT! ONE OF MY PLAYERS WANTS TO TALK TO ME...
© 1993 United Feature Syndicate, Inc.
THEY'RE HAVING A CONFERENCE, AREN'T THEY? THEY'RE PLANNING SOME CLEVER STRATEGY.. I JUST FEEL IT...
6-28
NO, LAST NIGHT YOU HAD YOUR SUPPER IN THE RED DISH AND WATER IN THE YELLOW DISH..
SCHULZ

CRACK!
© 1993 United Feature Syndicate, Inc.
HE HIT IT! CHARLIE BROWN HIT IT! THE BALL IS GOING TO THE FENCE! RUN, CHARLIE BROWN! RUN!
OH, NO! THE WORLD IS COMING TO AN END! I ALWAYS KNEW IT WOULD END THIS WAY!
6-29
SCHULZ

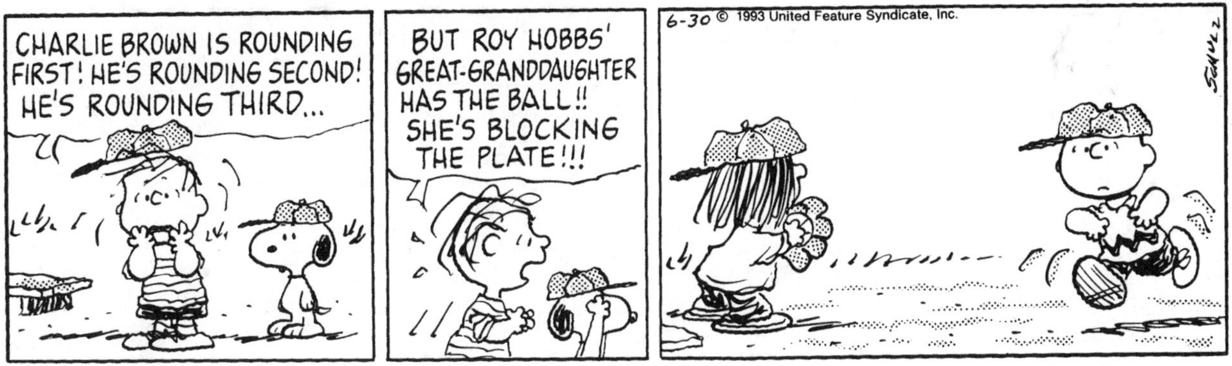
CHARLIE BROWN IS ROUNDING FIRST! HE'S ROUNDING SECOND! HE'S ROUNDING THIRD...
BUT ROY HOBBS' GREAT-GRANDDAUGHTER HAS THE BALL!! SHE'S BLOCKING THE PLATE!!!
6-30 © 1993 United Feature Syndicate, Inc.
SCHULZ

SLIDE, CHARLIE BROWN, SLIDE!!
© 1993 United Feature Syndicate, Inc.
7-1
SCHULZ

YOU DID IT, CHARLIE BROWN! YOU HIT ANOTHER HOME RUN, AND WE WON THE GAME!
YOU MEAN I WAS SAFE?
I'M ROY HOBBS' GREAT-GRANDDAUGHTER.. WHERE AM I? WHAT HAPPENED?
YOU WERE BLOCKING THE PLATE, SWEETIE.. HERE, I COULD ONLY FIND ONE SHOE..
7-2 © 1993 United Feature Syndicate, Inc.
SCHULZ

WELL, YOU DID IT AGAIN, DIDN'T YOU? YOU HIT ANOTHER HOME RUN, AND RUINED MY LIFE!
I WAS LUCKY
© 1993 United Feature Syndicate, Inc.
YOU ALMOST KILLED ME WHEN YOU SLID INTO HOME..
YOU WERE BLOCKING THE PLATE, SWEETIE..
I STILL CAN'T FIND MY OTHER SHOE...
I'M SORRY
7-3
I HATE GOING THE REST OF MY LIFE WEARING ONLY ONE SHOE
SCHULZ

THIS WOULD BE A MUCH BETTER WORLD IF DOGS COULD FLY, TOO..
7-5
IMAGINE A WARM SUMMER NIGHT...
© 1993 United Feature Syndicate, Inc.
AND OVERHEAD, A SKY FILLED WITH DOGS BARKING
SCHULZ

YOU KNOW HOW EVERYONE LIKES TO SEE GEESE FLYING ACROSS THE FACE OF A FULL MOON?
7-6
IF DOGS COULD FLY, WOULDN'T IT BE NEAT TO LOOK UP AND SEE A SAINT BERNARD FLYING ACROSS THE FACE OF THE MOON?
© 1993 United Feature Syndicate, Inc.
WELL, MAYBE NOT..
SCHULZ

PEANUTS®
by SCHULZ
YAWN

Z
Z
Z
Z
7-4
© 1993 United Feature Syndicate, Inc.
Z
Z

Z
Z
SCHULZ
Z
Z

ARE YOU AWAKE?
WHO WANTS TO KNOW?
7-7
I'M YOUR BROTHER... REMEMBER ME?
DO YOU HAVE ANY IDENTIFICATION?
SCHULZ

7-8
YES, I AGREE..IT TAKES COURAGE TO SAIL IN UNCHARTED WATERS..

I'M NOT SURE I WANT TO GO TO CAMP..
WELL, YOU'D BETTER MAKE UP YOUR MIND...THE BUS LEAVES IN FIVE MINUTES!
7-9
© 1993 United Feature Syndicate, Inc.
I'LL BE THERE IN SIX MINUTES..

NO, SIR.. MY SISTER WON'T BE COMING TO CAMP THIS YEAR..SHE MISSED THE BUS...BUT **I'M** HERE!
YES, SIR.. A YEAR AGO.. LAST PLACE IN THE SACK RACE..UH HUH.. THAT WAS ME..
7-10
© 1993 United Feature Syndicate, Inc.
SCHULZ
NO, I UNDERSTAND...YOU HAVE A LOT OF CAMPERS COME THROUGH HERE..

CALLING HOME, CHARLIE BROWN?
I THOUGHT I'D LET EVERYONE KNOW THAT I GOT HERE TO CAMP SAFELY..
"THANK YOU FOR CALLING THE BROWN RESIDENCE.. IF YOU KNOW THE FOUR DIGIT EXTENSION OF THE PARTY YOU ARE TRYING TO REACH, YOU MAY DIAL IT NOW..IF YOU ARE CALLING YOUR SISTER, PRESS THREE..IF YOU HAVE A ROTARY DIAL TELEPHONE, PLEASE HOLD FOR THE NEXT AVAILABLE PERSON..."
© 1993 United Feature Syndicate, Inc.
SCHULZ
7-12

HELLO? OH, IS THIS YOU, BIG BROTHER?
YOU'RE AT CAMP, AND I'M NOT!
HA HA HA HA HA!!
NEVER CALL HOME!
© 1993 United Feature Syndicate, Inc.
SCHULZ
7-13

HI! MY NAME IS ETHAN.. I JUST GOT BACK FROM "CRAFTS"
WE'VE BEEN LEARNING HOW TO MAKE BOWS AND ARROWS LIKE THE INDIANS..
7-14
© 1993 United Feature Syndicate, Inc.
THIS IS THE ARROW I MADE..
THAT'S AN INDIAN ARROW?
SURE, WITHOUT IT, THEY WOULDN'T KNOW WHICH WAY THEY WERE GOING..
SCHULZ

WHAT DO YOU WANT TO BE WHEN YOU GROW UP, ETHAN?
A NEWSPAPER COLUMNIST..
© 1993 United Feature Syndicate, Inc.
I HAVE VERY STRONG OPINIONS ABOUT EVERYTHING
7-15
THAT'S A STUPID LOOKING SHIRT YOU'RE WEARING..
SCHULZ

CARL SAGAN SAYS THERE ARE A HUNDRED BILLION STARS IN OUR GALAXY, AND THERE ARE A HUNDRED BILLION GALAXIES, AND EACH GALAXY CONTAINS A HUNDRED BILLION STARS! SORT OF PUTS THINGS IN PERSPECTIVE, DOESN'T IT CHARLIE BROWN?
I MISS MY DOG..
© 1993 United Feature Syndicate, Inc.
7-16
SCHULZ

HI, SALLY.. I'M COMING HOME THIS AFTERNOON...
HAS MY DOG MISSED ME?
7-17
OH, YES..HE'S BEEN WAITING FOR YOU...
© 1993 United Feature Syndicate, Inc.
WELCOME HOME, ROUND-HEADED KID!
SCHULZ

I KNOW IT'S HOT, MEN, BUT LET'S KEEP GOING..
NOT TOO FAR AHEAD IS AN OASIS WHERE THERE'LL BE LOTS OF WATER...
© 1993 United Feature Syndicate, Inc.
7-19
SCHULZ

7-20
© 1993 United Feature Syndicate, Inc.
IT IS SAID THAT WHEN DOGS DRINK FROM THE RIVER NILE, THEY DO IT WHILE RUNNING SO AS NOT TO BE SEIZED BY CROCODILES..
I FEEL RIDICULOUS
SCHULZ

7-21
JUST SPIT THEM OUT..
THOSE ARE BUTTONS..THEY KEEP THE WATERMELON FROM FALLING APART..
© 1993 United Feature Syndicate, Inc.
HE NEVER BELIEVES ANYTHING I TELL HIM
SCHULZ

FALLING ROCK
© 1993 United Feature Syndicate, Inc.
7-22
FALLING THINGS
SCHULZ

SO HERE I AM LEFT TO GUARD THE CAR WHILE THE FAMILY GOES SHOPPING..
7-23
ANYONE WHO COMES NEAR THIS VEHICLE WILL MEET A SNARLING TORNADO!
© 1993 United Feature Syndicate, Inc.
ON THE OTHER HAND, FOR TWO COOKIES THEY CAN HAVE THE CAR..
SCHULZ

7-24 © 1993 United Feature Syndicate, Inc.
SCHULZ

PEANUTS
by SCHULZ

THIS IS KIND OF INTERESTING
"SOMETIMES WHEN A DOG IS ABOUT TO GO TO SLEEP, IT WILL TURN AROUND IN A CIRCLE BEFORE LYING DOWN.."
"THIS HABIT GOES BACK TO THE DOG'S WILD ANCESTORS WHO STAMPED DOWN THE GRASS TO FORM A NESTLIKE BED.."
© 1993 United Feature Syndicate, Inc.
7-25
WHAT DOES IT SAY ABOUT WAKING UP?
SCHULZ

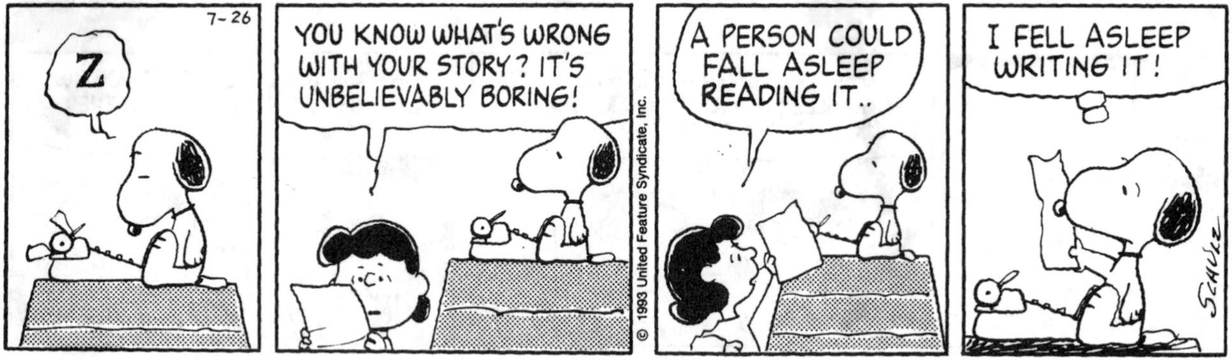
7-26
Z
YOU KNOW WHAT'S WRONG WITH YOUR STORY? IT'S UNBELIEVABLY BORING!
© 1993 United Feature Syndicate, Inc.
A PERSON COULD FALL ASLEEP READING IT..
I FELL ASLEEP WRITING IT!
SCHULZ

I THINK YOU TAKE THIS GAME TOO SERIOUSLY, CHARLIE BROWN...
7-27
YOU PUT TOO MUCH STRESS ON YOURSELF..
YOU'RE PROBABLY RIGHT, LUCY.. THANKS FOR REMINDING ME..
© 1993 United Feature Syndicate, Inc.
TRY TO GET THE BALL OVER THE PLATE! YOU THINK WE'RE OUT HERE FOR THE FUN OF IT?!
SCHULZ

OKAY, SHOOT!
7-29
© 1993 United Feature Syndicate, Inc.
YOU DIDN'T SAY, "NICE TRY"
SCHULZ

GUESS WHAT, MARCIE.. I'VE BEEN DOING A LITTLE SUMMER READING..
MAYBE YOU CAN HELP ME.. WHY DID VANNA WHITE TAKE THE CARAMELED APPLE FROM THE WITCH?
© 1993 United Feature Syndicate, Inc.
"SNOW" WHITE, SIR.. AND IT WAS A PLAIN APPLE..
7-30
PRETTY PROFOUND STORY, HUH, MARCIE?
SCHULZ

PSYCHIATRIC HELP 5¢
THE DOCTOR IS IN
HOW DO I KNOW IF THE ADVICE YOU'RE GOING TO GIVE ME WILL BE ANY GOOD?
7-31
ANY ADVICE YOU GET HERE IS GUARANTEED TO BE RIGHT ON TARGET..
THE DOCTOR IS IN
ALL RIGHT, I'LL TAKE A CHANCE...
© 1993 United Feature Syndicate, Inc.
SIT UP STRAIGHT! YOU'RE SLOUCHING!
THE DOCTOR IS IN
SCHULZ

DO YOU THINK IT'S POSSIBLE TO RIDE CLEAR ACROSS THE LAKE ON A BEACH BALL?
I DOUBT IT, WHY?
I WAS JUST WONDERING..
SCHULZ
© 1993 United Feature Syndicate, Inc. 8-2

DEAR GRANDMA, I AM DICTATING THIS LETTER TO MY SISTER SALLY WHO IS STUDYING SHORTHAND...
8-3
MAYBE YOU'D BETTER JUST CALL HER ON THE PHONE..
SCHULZ
© 1993 United Feature Syndicate, Inc.

SOMETIMES I LIE AWAKE AT NIGHT, AND I ASK MYSELF, "IS THIS ALL THERE IS?"
THEN I HEAR A VOICE THAT SAYS..
"WHAT KIND OF A QUESTION IS THAT?"
8-4
SCHULZ
© 1993 United Feature Syndicate, Inc.

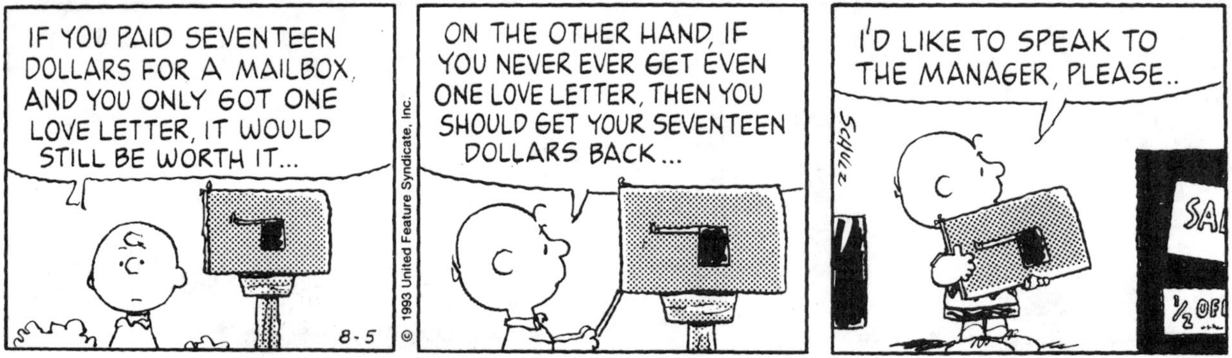
IF YOU PAID SEVENTEEN DOLLARS FOR A MAILBOX, AND YOU ONLY GOT ONE LOVE LETTER, IT WOULD STILL BE WORTH IT...
8-5
© 1993 United Feature Syndicate, Inc.
ON THE OTHER HAND, IF YOU NEVER EVER GET EVEN ONE LOVE LETTER, THEN YOU SHOULD GET YOUR SEVENTEEN DOLLARS BACK...
I'D LIKE TO SPEAK TO THE MANAGER, PLEASE..
SCHULZ

DID YOU KNOW OUR NAME IS IN THE PHONE BOOK?
© 1993 United Feature Syndicate, Inc.
SEE? THERE'S OUR NAME, OUR ADDRESS AND OUR PHONE NUMBER...
8-6
YOU NEVER TOLD ME WE WERE FAMOUS..
SCHULZ

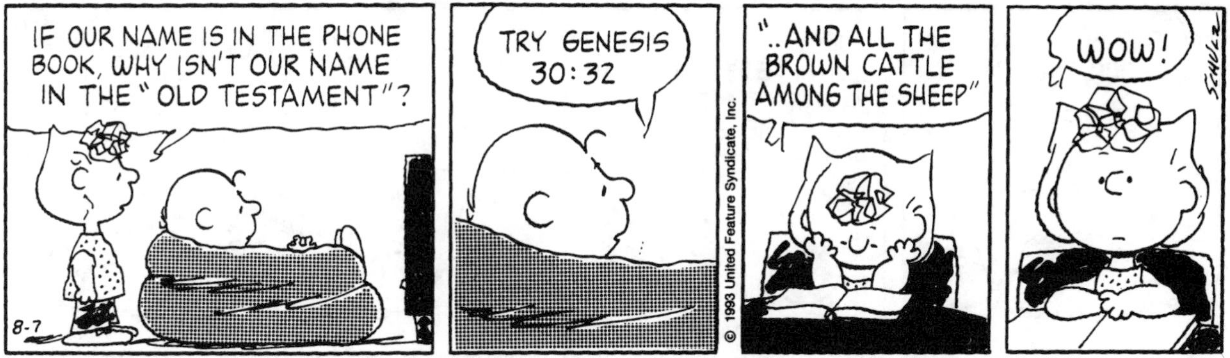
8-7
IF OUR NAME IS IN THE PHONE BOOK, WHY ISN'T OUR NAME IN THE "OLD TESTAMENT"?
TRY GENESIS 30:32
"..AND ALL THE BROWN CATTLE AMONG THE SHEEP"
WOW!
SCHULZ
© 1993 United Feature Syndicate, Inc.

YOU ARE MY YOUNGER BROTHER AND I AM YOUR OLDER SISTER, AND THAT'S THE WAY IT'S GOING TO BE ALL THE DAYS OF YOUR LIFE..
© 1993 United Feature Syndicate, Inc.
8-9
..AND DON'T TELL ME YOU NEVER THINK ABOUT IT..
SCHULZ

THE SUN IS IN YOUR EYES?
WELL, PUT ON SOME SUNGLASSES, OR WEAR A HAT OR SIT UNDER AN UMBRELLA..
© 1993 United Feature Syndicate, Inc.
8-10
..OR DO ALL THREE..
SCHULZ

YES, MA'AM.. DO YOU HAVE ANY BOOKS HERE IN YOUR LIBRARY WHERE A DOG TAKES OVER THE WHOLE WORLD?
© 1993 United Feature Syndicate, Inc.
SCHULZ
8-11
WELL, I THINK NOW YOU'VE GOT ONE..

SCHOOL STARTS IN FOUR WEEKS!!
© 1993 United Feature Syndicate, Inc.
DETAILS AT ELEVEN..
8-12
SCHULZ

YES, SIR.. WE'D LIKE TO BUY SOME SCHOOL SUPPLIES
© 1993 United Feature Syndicate, Inc.
THINGS LIKE PAPER AND PENCILS..
8-13
AND LOTS OF ERASERS..
SCHULZ

PEANUTS®
by SCHULZ

8-15
© 1993 United Feature Syndicate, Inc.
WHY CAN'T I HAVE A NORMAL DOG LIKE EVERYONE ELSE?
SCHULZ

YES, SIR.. YOU WANT TO KNOW WHY WE'RE BUYING OUR SCHOOL SUPPLIES SO EARLY?
TELL HIM WE'RE TRYING TO CREATE THE ILLUSION THAT WE'RE ANXIOUS TO BECOME EDUCATED..
WE JUST LIKE TO BE PREPARED
8-14
© 1993 United Feature Syndicate, Inc.
MY ANSWER WAS BETTER
SCHULZ

NOW, GET OUT THERE IN RIGHT FIELD, AND CONCENTRATE!
THINK ABOUT WHAT YOU'RE DOING..
KEEP YOUR MIND ON THE GAME..
8-16
© 1993 United Feature Syndicate, Inc.
KEEP YOUR HEAD OUT OF THE CLOUDS..
SCHULZ

ROYANNE! WHAT A SURPRISE!
I NEED TO TALK TO YOU, CHARLES..DO YOU HAVE TIME TO GO GET A CHOCOLATE SUNDAE?
8-17
© 1993 United Feature Syndicate, Inc.
OKAY, ROYANNE, WHAT'S UP?
DO YOU LIKE ME, CHARLES?
OH, GOOD GRIEF!
SCHULZ

I HAVE TO TELL YOU SOMETHING, CHARLES.. BUT FIRST, I WANT TO KNOW IF YOU LIKE ME...
WELL, SURE, I LIKE YOU, ROYANNE.. BUT I DON'T REALLY KNOW YOU..I MEAN, OUR TEAM PLAYED YOUR TEAM A COUPLE OF TIMES..
© 1993 United Feature Syndicate, Inc.
AND, OF COURSE, I HIT THOSE TWO HOME RUNS, AND..
8-18
THAT'S WHAT I HAVE TO CONFESS, CHARLES..I COULD HAVE STRUCK YOU OUT IF I HAD WANTED TO!
SCHULZ

YOU LET ME HIT THOSE HOME RUNS?!
8-19
© 1993 United Feature Syndicate, Inc.
I HAD TO, CHARLES..YOU LOOKED CUTE STANDING THERE AT THE PLATE..
I DIDN'T WANT TO LOOK CUTE!!
HOW ABOUT PATHETIC?
I CAN'T STAND IT!
SCHULZ

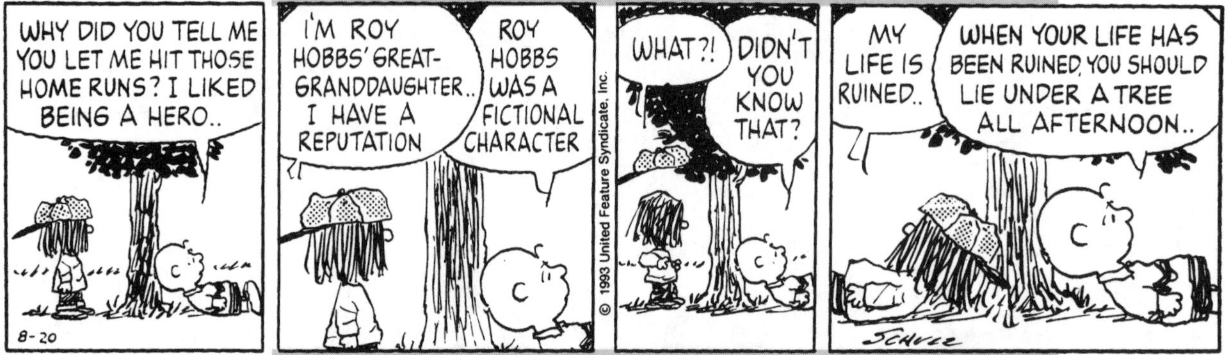
WHY DID YOU TELL ME YOU LET ME HIT THOSE HOME RUNS? I LIKED BEING A HERO..
8-20
© 1993 United Feature Syndicate, Inc.
I'M ROY HOBBS' GREAT-GRANDDAUGHTER.. I HAVE A REPUTATION
ROY HOBBS WAS A FICTIONAL CHARACTER
© 1993 United Feature Syndicate, Inc.
WHAT?!
DIDN'T YOU KNOW THAT?
MY LIFE IS RUINED..
WHEN YOUR LIFE HAS BEEN RUINED, YOU SHOULD LIE UNDER A TREE ALL AFTERNOON..
SCHULZ

SHE ASKED YOU TO GO OUT FOR A CHOCOLATE SUNDAE?
UH HUH.. AND THEN SHE CONFESSED THAT SHE HAD LET ME HIT THOSE HOME RUNS! I WAS CRUSHED!
8-21
© 1993 United Feature Syndicate, Inc.
I WAS HUMILIATED!
AND THEN SHE LET ME PAY FOR THE CHOCOLATE SUNDAES!
SCHULZ

HORSES ARE RELATIVELY EASY TO TRAIN..MULES ARE EASIER TO TRAIN THAN DONKEYS..IT TAKES PATIENCE TO TRAIN A DONKEY...A MULE IS ONE-HALF DONKEY AND ONE-HALF HORSE..
DON'T ALWAYS FEEL IT'S NECESSARY TO MAKE CONVERSATION, MARCIE..
8-23
© 1993 United Feature Syndicate, Inc.
SCHULZ

MISS DAVIS IS GOING TO BE SURPRISED WHEN SHE GETS THIS BOOK REPORT..
MISS DAVIS QUIT TEACHING TWO YEARS AGO..SHE GOT MARRIED, AND HAS A NEW BABY
© 1993 United Feature Syndicate, Inc.
MAYBE I COULD ATTACH A "CONGRATULATIONS" CARD TO THE REPORT..
8/24

YOU KNOW WHAT WE SHOULD DO, MARCIE? WE SHOULD SIGN UP FOR RIDING LESSONS..
ON HORSES?
© 1993 United Feature Syndicate, Inc.
THERE AREN'T ANY ZEBRAS AROUND HERE, MARCIE..
8-25

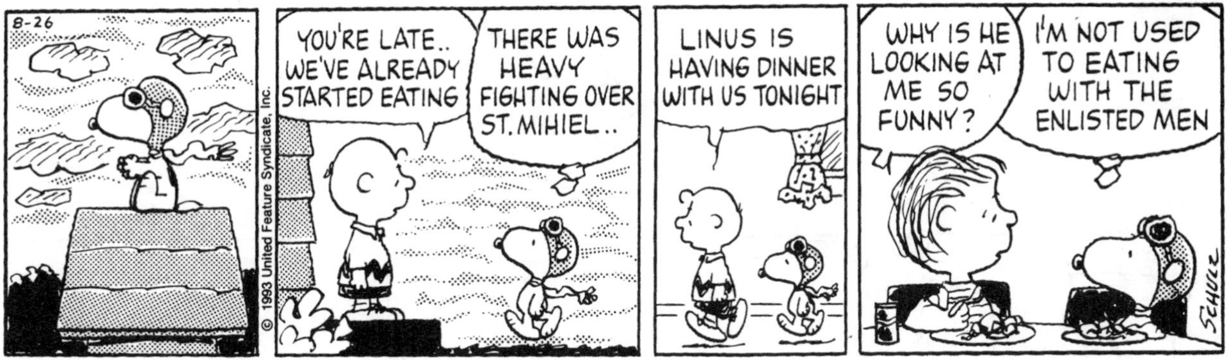
8-26
YOU'RE LATE.. WE'VE ALREADY STARTED EATING
THERE WAS HEAVY FIGHTING OVER ST. MIHIEL..
© 1993 United Feature Syndicate, Inc.
LINUS IS HAVING DINNER WITH US TONIGHT
WHY IS HE LOOKING AT ME SO FUNNY?
I'M NOT USED TO EATING WITH THE ENLISTED MEN
SCHULZ

IF YOU'RE GOING TO BE FLYING OVER PARIS, COULD I HITCH A RIDE?
8-27
IT'S AGAINST REGULATIONS, BUT I SUPPOSE WE CAN DO IT..
© 1993 United Feature Syndicate, Inc.
IS IT VERY FAR?
NO, THERE'S PARIS NOW..
HAVE A GOOD TIME!
SCHULZ

PEANUTS
by SCHULZ

8-29
© 1993 United Feature Syndicate, Inc.

HEY, CHUCK..YOUR CRAZY DOG ALMOST KILLED ME!
8/28
POOR GIRL..WE WERE FLYING OVER PARIS AND SHE FELL OUT OF THE PLANE..
FORTUNATELY, WE WERE FLYING VERY LOW
YOU SHOULD DO SOMETHING ABOUT THAT DOG, CHUCK..
© 1993 United Feature Syndicate, Inc.
CIVILIANS SHOULDN'T BE ALLOWED ON THE AËRODROME..
SCHULZ

I'VE ALWAYS WONDERED WHY BIRDS FLY IN A "V" FORMATION...
© 1993 United Feature Syndicate, Inc.
8-30
YOUR MOM TOLD YOU TO ?
SCHULZ

SCHOOL STARTS NEXT WEEK.. I NEED YOU TO TEST ME ON MY MULTIPLICATION TABLES...
OKAY, HOW MUCH IS FIVE TIMES EIGHT?
© 1993 United Feature Syndicate, Inc.
WHO CARES?
I THINK YOU'RE READY
SCHULZ
9-1

TOO BIG FOR YOU? ALL RIGHT, BRING YOUR OWN BALL..
9-2
© 1993 United Feature Syndicate, Inc.
WHAT HAPPENS IF I SWALLOW IT?
SCHULZ

9-3
WHEE!
© 1993 United Feature Syndicate, Inc.
IT'S HARD TO EXPLAIN WHY BALLOONS ARE SO MUCH FUN
SCHULZ

HI! I GUESS YOU KNOW THAT SCHOOL STARTS NEXT WEEK..
© 1993 United Feature Syndicate, Inc.
BEFORE YOU KNOW IT, THOUSANDS OF SCREAMING KIDS WILL BE RUNNING THROUGH YOUR HALLS!
9-4
JUST THINKING ABOUT IT GIVES ME ROOM-ACHE!
SCHULZ

SCHOOL STARTS TOMORROW!!
WOULD YOU RECOGNIZE THE PRINCIPAL IF YOU MET HIM ON THE STREET ?! BE READY! BE READY!
9-6
© 1993 United Feature Syndicate, Inc.

AFTER I GRADUATE FROM SCHOOL, WILL I BE A BETTER PERSON?
PROBABLY.. A GOOD EDUCATION IS VERY IMPORTANT
THAT'S RIGHT.. LEARNING ALWAYS MAKES YOU A BETTER PERSON..
UNLESS YOU DON'T HAVE A DOG..
9-7
© 1993 United Feature Syndicate, Inc.

9-8
Z
YES, MA'AM..
I'M AWAKE!
© 1993 United Feature Syndicate, Inc.
DO I HAVE ANYTHING
TO TELL THE CLASS?
YES, MA'AM..
THERE'S A SPIDER
ON THE CEILING..
SCHULZ

HEY, MARCIE, WE DON'T
HAVE ANY HOMEWORK
TONIGHT, DO WE? WE **DO**?!
PAGE SIXTEEN?
PAGE SIXTEEN
OF WHAT?
© 1993 United Feature Syndicate, Inc.
A BOOK?
WHAT BOOK?
9-9
DON'T HANG
UP, MARCIE..
SCHULZ

HERE, I NEED YOU TO TEST ME ON THESE HISTORICAL DATES..
© 1993 United Feature Syndicate, Inc.
IN WHAT YEAR DID THE VISIGOTHS CROSS THE DANUBE?
9-11
WHO CARES?
I'VE ALWAYS BEEN GOOD WITH HISTORICAL DATES..
SCHULZ

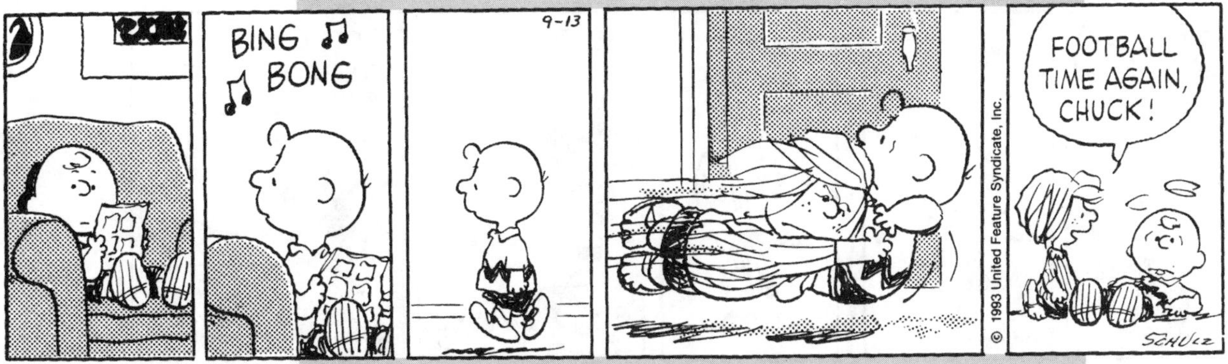
BING
BONG
9-13
© 1993 United Feature Syndicate, Inc.
FOOTBALL TIME AGAIN, CHUCK!
SCHULZ

GO STRAIGHT DOWN THE FIELD, MARCIE, CUT LEFT, AND I'LL HIT YOU..
9-14
© 1993 United Feature Syndicate, Inc.
HIT ME WITH WHAT ?
SCHULZ

I'LL RUN DOWN THE FIELD, MARCIE, AND YOU THROW ME THE BALL..
9-15
© 1993 United Feature Syndicate, Inc.
?
MARCIE! WHERE DID YOU GO?!
AFTER YOU RAN DOWN THE FIELD, I SUDDENLY FELT VERY LONELY..
SCHULZ

ARE YOU READY?
9-16
© 1993 United Feature Syndicate, Inc.
I'M READY, MARCIE, BUT BEFORE YOU KICK THE BALL, SQUEEZE IT A FEW TIMES...
WHAT IF IT BECOMES FOND OF ME?
SCHULZ

MY DAD BOUGHT ME THIS HELMET, SIR.. HE SAYS GIRLS CAN PLAY SPORTS JUST AS WELL AS BOYS CAN..
9-17
© 1993 United Feature Syndicate, Inc.
I TRIED IT IN THE POOL, AND I ALMOST DROWNED..
SCHULZ

9-18
YOU THINK YOU'RE VERY CLEVER, DON'T YOU?
© 1993 United Feature Syndicate, Inc.
SCHULZ

© 1993 United Feature Syndicate, Inc.
SCHOOL STARTED LAST WEEK!!
9-20
I WASN'T SURE YOU HAD NOTICED
SCHULZ

MY DAD TOOK ME TO MY FIRST HOCKEY GAME LAST NIGHT..
IT WAS REALLY GREAT..
I LOVED WATCHING THE ZAMBONI GO AROUND..
YOU'RE VERY WEIRD, MARCIE..
SCHULZ
© 1993 United Feature Syndicate, Inc.
9-21

GRAMMA SAYS THAT JUST BEFORE SHE GOES TO SLEEP EACH NIGHT, SHE HEARS ANGELS SINGING..
I HEARD SOMETHING LIKE THAT MYSELF LAST NIGHT...
YOU HEARD ANGELS SINGING?
NO, MY DOG WANTED TO COME IN..
SCHULZ
© 1993 United Feature Syndicate, Inc.
9-22

I CAN'T REMEMBER MY LOCKER COMBINATION
9-23
© 1993 United Feature Syndicate, Inc.
WE DON'T HAVE LOCKERS IN OUR SCHOOL..
U.S. MAIL
THAT WAS ANOTHER THING I COULDN'T REMEMBER

I KNOW YOU'RE THINKING OF GRABBING THIS BLANKET, AND DRAGGING ME ALL OVER THE NEIGHBORHOOD
THEREFORE, I WOULD SUGGEST YOU PUT THAT THOUGHT IN THE DEEPEST RECESS OF YOUR MIND..
9-24
© 1993 United Feature Syndicate, Inc.
DOGS' MINDS DON'T HAVE RECESSES!

9-25
FINESSE!
© 1993 United Feature Syndicate, Inc.

9-27
MY DAD TOOK ME TO ANOTHER HOCKEY GAME LAST NIGHT..
I GOT TO MEET THE MAN WHO DRIVES THE ZUCCHINI..
ZAMBONI..
WHATEVER
© 1993 United Feature Syndicate, Inc.

I'M AWAKE!
BUT I CAN'T GET DRESSED RIGHT AWAY..
MY SOCKS ARE STILL SLEEPING
9-28
© 1993 United Feature Syndicate, Inc.
SCHULZ

9-29
Z
Z
Z
Z
Z
U.S. MAIL
WHY DO I HAVE THE FEELING THE SCHOOL BUS HAS BROKEN DOWN AGAIN?
BUS STOP
© 1993 United Feature Syndicate, Inc.
SCHULZ

I THINK I'LL ASK THE TEACHER IF I CAN MOVE MY DESK NEXT TO THAT LITTLE RED-HAIRED GIRL..
9-30
THEN, ONE DAY I CAN REACH OVER AND TOUCH HER HAND..
© 1993 United Feature Syndicate, Inc.
AND SHE CAN LOOK AT ME LIKE I'VE LOST MY MIND!
MAYBE I'LL ASK THE TEACHER IF I CAN MOVE MY DESK OUT INTO THE HALLWAY..

OKAY, MARCIE, WHEN I COME RUNNING DOWN THE FIELD, YOU TRY TO STOP ME..
AND DON'T FORGET TO USE YOUR HELMET..
10-1
© 1993 United Feature Syndicate, Inc.
BONK!
THANKS FOR THE SUGGESTION, SIR!

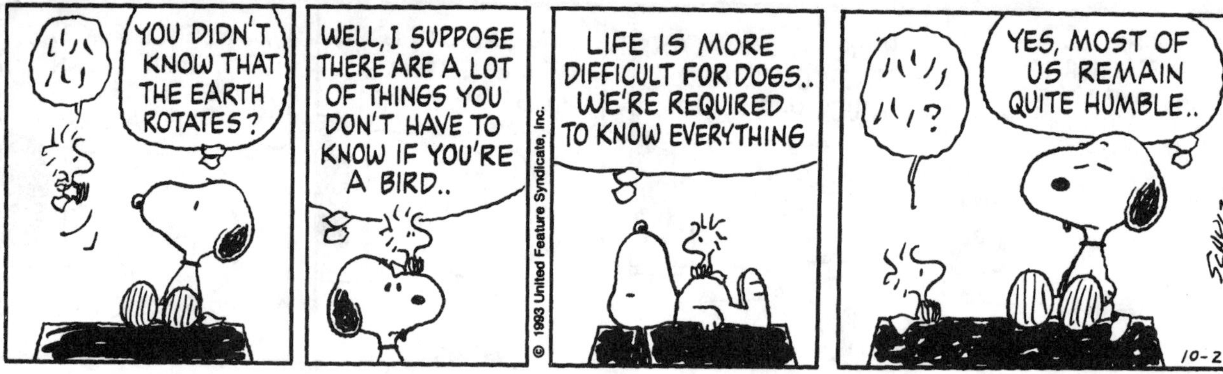
YOU DIDN'T KNOW THAT THE EARTH ROTATES?
WELL, I SUPPOSE THERE ARE A LOT OF THINGS YOU DON'T HAVE TO KNOW IF YOU'RE A BIRD..
LIFE IS MORE DIFFICULT FOR DOGS.. WE'RE REQUIRED TO KNOW EVERYTHING
?
YES, MOST OF US REMAIN QUITE HUMBLE..
© 1993 United Feature Syndicate, Inc.
SCHULZ
10-2

© 1993 United Feature Syndicate, Inc.
10-4
PLEASE, YOU DON'T HAVE TO TELL ME EVERY LITTLE DETAIL!
SCHULZ

YES, MA'AM.. THE ANSWER IS "TWELVE"
IT IS? I WAS RIGHT?
TAKE IT EASY, MA'AM..
SPLASH A LITTLE COLD WATER ON YOUR FACE, AND YOU'LL FEEL BETTER..
10-5
© 1993 United Feature Syndicate, Inc.
SCHULZ

IF YOU REALLY LOVED ME, YOU'D BUY ME A MUSIC BOX..
IF YOU REALLY LOVED ME, YOU WOULDN'T ASK ME TO BUY YOU A MUSIC BOX..
ANOTHER TIE
10-6
© 1993 United Feature Syndicate, Inc.
SCHULZ

I THINK A MUSIC BOX IS THE MOST ROMANTIC GIFT THAT A BOY CAN GIVE TO A GIRL..
HOW ABOUT HALF OF A PEANUT BUTTER SANDWICH?
© 1993 United Feature Syndicate, Inc.
10-7
WHAT SONG DOES IT PLAY?
SCHULZ

A MUSIC BOX! LINUS, YOU BOUGHT ME A MUSIC BOX!
WELL, YOU SAID A MUSIC BOX IS THE MOST ROMANTIC GIFT THAT A BOY CAN GIVE TO A GIRL..
10-8
© 1993 United Feature Syndicate, Inc.
IT IS! IT'S VERY SPECIAL..
I'LL PUT IT WITH ALL THE OTHERS
SCHULZ

10-9
© 1993 United Feature Syndicate, Inc.
OKAY, GO LEAN ON A CAT!
SCHULZ

I NEED YOU TO WRITE A THEME FOR ME..
© 1993 United Feature Syndicate, Inc.
IF YOU DON'T WRITE IT YOURSELF, HOW WILL YOU EVER LEARN?
10-11
LEARN?
SCHULZ

Dear Brother Snoopy,
Life here on the desert is exciting.
10-12
Last night the sun went down and this morning the sun came up.
© 1993 United Feature Syndicate, Inc.
There's always something happening.
SCHULZ

IF EVERYONE LISTENED TO ME, THIS WOULD BE A PERFECT WORLD!
JUST THINK ABOUT IT.. WOULDN'T YOU LOVE TO LIVE IN A PERFECT WORLD?
© 1993 United Feature Syndicate, Inc.
10-13
WELL, WHY NOT?!
SCHULZ

© 1993 United Feature Syndicate, Inc.
HAS THE SCHOOL BUS COME YET?
U.S. MAIL
I CAN'T TELL.. SOMEBODY'S FOOT IS IN MY FACE..
10-14

Z
© 1993 United Feature Syndicate, Inc.
AFRICA! SIXTEEN! SHAKESPEARE! ALABAMA! THE RIVER NILE!
10-15
WERE ANY OF THOSE RIGHT, MA'AM? I COULD TELL HER WHEN SHE WAKES UP AGAIN..
Z

I'M READY, SIR..
LET'S GO OUT AND KICK THAT BALL AROUND ON THE OL' GRIDLOCK!
GRIDIRON, MARCIE..
WHATEVER
© 1993 United Feature Syndicate, Inc.
10-16
SCHULZ

SOMEDAY I WANT TO GO OVER TO JERICHO, AND WATCH THE WALLS COME TUMBLING DOWN
I THINK YOU'RE ABOUT THREE THOUSAND YEARS TOO LATE..
RATS! NOBODY EVER TELLS ME ANYTHING!
© 1993 United Feature Syndicate, Inc.
10-18
SCHULZ

NOTHING IS MORE EMPTY THAN AN EMPTY MAILBOX..
IF YOU PUT YOUR EAR UP REAL CLOSE, YOU CAN HEAR THE OCEAN ROAR..
10-19
© 1993 United Feature Syndicate, Inc.
SCHULZ

I THINK SOUNDS ARE INTERESTING, DON'T YOU?
WHAT IS YOUR FAVORITE SOUND?
KLUNK
"KLUNK"? YES, "KLUNK" IS A VERY INTERESTING SOUND..
10-20
© 1993 United Feature Syndicate, Inc.
SCHULZ

SIR, INSTEAD OF PLAYING, MAYBE I SHOULD JUST BE A CHEERLEADER..
LISTEN TO THIS...
COME ON, TEAM! TRY TO DO YOUR VERY BEST!!
LET'S JUST WORK ON SOME MORE PLAYS, MARCIE
A LITTLE TOO IMPASSIONED, HUH?
10-21
© 1993 United Feature Syndicate, Inc.

"FIGHT, FIGHT, FIGHT WITH ALL YOUR MIGHT, AND GO ON TO A HIGHER HEIGHT!"
MARCIE, THAT'S THE WORST CHEER I'VE EVER HEARD!
I HAD HOPED IT WOULD BE INSPIRATIONAL, SIR..
IT'LL INSPIRE EVERYONE TO GO HOME..
HOW ABOUT, "TURN OUT THE LIGHTS, LUNCH IS OVER"?
10-22
© 1993 United Feature Syndicate, Inc.

HEY, CHUCK.. I WAS WONDERING IF YOU NEED A CHEERLEADER FOR YOUR FOOTBALL TEAM..
© 1993 United Feature Syndicate, Inc.
STUPID MARCIE HERE THINKS SHE CAN BE A CHEERLEADER..
SORRY, I ALREADY HAVE ONE..
"WOOF WOOF! ARF ARF! LET'S GET 'EM IN THE SECOND HARF!"
SCHULZ
10-23

10-25
THIS GAME IS GOING INTO OVERTIME..
IT MUST BE MIDNIGHT WHERE THEY'RE PLAYING..
I'M SURPRISED THE CROWD IS STILL THERE..
THEY SHOULD GO HOME AND FEED THEIR DOG..
SCHULZ
© 1993 United Feature Syndicate, Inc.

I GOT A "C," AN "A," AN "R" AND A "D"! ..NOT TOO BAD, HUH, MARCIE?
THAT'S "CARD," SIR... IT SAYS "REPORT CARD"
I WAS WONDERING HOW I GOT AN "R"...
© 1993 United Feature Syndicate, Inc.
10/26

THE LOCH NESS PUTTER!
© 1993 United Feature Syndicate, Inc.
10-27

WHERE ARE YOU GOING?
OUT TO MAKE MONEY RAKING LEAVES..
10-28
I'M GOING TO USE SALESMANSHIP..I'LL CONVINCE EVERYONE THEY NEED THEIR LEAVES RAKED!
© 1993 United Feature Syndicate, Inc.
IT'S ALL A MATTER OF SALESMANSHIP, PERSEVERANCE AND BEING WELL LIKED..
WILLY LOMAN OF THE LEAVES
SCHULZ

ASK YOUR DAD IF HE WANTS ME TO RAKE YOUR LEAVES..
10-29
© 1993 United Feature Syndicate, Inc.
HE SAYS, "HOW MUCH FOR JUST ONE LEAF?"
MY DAD THINKS HE'S VERY FUNNY
SCHULZ

PEANUTS
SCHULZ

NOW WHAT?

EXPLAIN TO ME WHAT I'M DOING OUT HERE..
ON HALLOWEEN NIGHT, THE "GREAT PUMPKIN" RISES OUT OF THE PUMPKIN PATCH, AND BRINGS TOYS TO ALL THE CHILDREN IN THE WORLD!
JUST THINK..IF HE CHOOSES THIS PUMPKIN PATCH, YOU AND I WILL BE HERE TO SEE HIM!
10-31
© 1993 United Feature Syndicate, Inc.

LOOK! THERE HE IS! IT'S THE "GREAT PUMPKIN"!
THAT'S NOT THE "GREAT PUMPKIN"... THAT'S A DOG HOLDING A PUMPKIN ON A STICK!
EXPLAIN TO ME AGAIN WHAT I'M DOING OUT HERE..
TRICK OR TREAT!
SCHULZ

HOW DID IT GO? DID YOU MAKE ANY MONEY DOING LEAVES?
NO, NOT A PENNY..
MAYBE I CAN TRY IT..COULD I BORROW YOUR CLUB?
RAKE
© 1993 United Feature Syndicate, Inc.
WHATEVER
10-30
OKAY, HERE'S HOW IT WORKS..I RENT YOU THE RAKE, SEE, AND..
SCHULZ

HERE'S THE WORLD WAR I FLYING ACE SITTING IN A SMALL FRENCH CAFE.. THE WAR DRAGS ON... HE IS DEPRESSED..
CHARLES, YOUR DOG IS IN OUR KITCHEN AGAIN DRINKING ALL OUR ROOT BEER..
11-1
© 1993 United Feature Syndicate, Inc.
GENERAL PERSHING SAYS FOR YOU TO GET BACK TO THE AERODROME RIGHT AWAY..
PRESSURE AGAIN FROM HEADQUARTERS, RAIN AND MUD,... DESPAIR...
MOM!
SCHULZ

HERE'S THE WORLD WAR I FLYING ACE WALKING BACK TO THE AERODROME..
SUDDENLY HE SEES A LIGHT IN THE WINDOW OF A SMALL SHABBY FARM HOUSE
11-2
HE TAPS GENTLY ON THE DOOR..
BAM! BAM! BAM!!
© 1993 United Feature Syndicate, Inc.
GO ON HOME, YOU STUPID BEAGLE!
SOMETIMES THE UNIFORM FRIGHTENS THEM..
SCHULZ

BEFORE HE GETS BACK TO THE AERODROME, THE FLYING ACE FEELS HE NEEDS ONE MORE ROOT BEER..
HE ENTERS ANOTHER SMALL SEEDY CAFE, AND BECKONS TO THE PLAIN LOOKING WAITRESS...
© 1993 United Feature Syndicate, Inc.
HEY, CHUCK! YOUR DOG JUST WALKED INTO OUR HOUSE..
11/3
WELL, YEAH, HE SEEMED TO WANT SOMETHING TO DRINK...I GAVE HIM WHAT WE HAD...
PRETTY CHEAP ROOT BEER..
SCHULZ

OKAY, FLYING ACE.. YOU'VE HAD ENOUGH... YOU'D BETTER GET GOING..
© 1993 United Feature Syndicate, Inc.
SMAK!
PATHETIC CREATURE..SHE SEEMED RATHER LONELY..
SCHULZ
11-4

I WAS PASSING BY THIS QUAINT JOINT, AND HEARD THE TINKLING OF A PIANO..
11-5
© 1993 United Feature Syndicate, Inc.
PLAY "TIPPERARY" FOR ME, SON.. I FEEL SORT OF DOWN TONIGHT...
SCHULZ

HI, CHARLES..DID YOUR DOG GET HOME ALL RIGHT?
11-6
SURE, CHARLIE BROWN, HE ALMOST KICKED OUR DOOR DOWN!
HEY, CHUCK, THAT'S A WEIRD DOG YOU'VE GOT THERE!
SO ALL I'M SAYING IS I DON'T WANT HIM LEANING ON MY PIANO..
© 1993 United Feature Syndicate, Inc.
WHY CAN'T I HAVE A NORMAL DOG LIKE EVERYONE ELSE?
WAS THAT GENERAL PERSHING? TELL HIM I'M ON MY WAY..
SCHULZ

IT IS DAWN.. HERE'S THE WORLD WAR I FLYING ACE WALKING ONTO THE AERODROME
11-8
HE CLIMBS INTO THE COCKPIT OF HIS SOPWITH CAMEL, AND ADJUSTS THE SUTTON HARNESS...
NOW, THE EARLY MORNING QUIET IS SHATTERED BY THE ROAR OF THE 110 HP LE RHÔNE ENGINE!
© 1993 United Feature Syndicate, Inc.
SCHULZ
SOME PEOPLE HAVE DOGS WHO BARK A LOT, OR DIG HOLES IN THE GARDEN, OR...

HERE'S THE WORLD WAR I FLYING ACE SEARCHING THE SKY FOR HIS ENEMY, THE RED BARON..
© 1993 United Feature Syndicate, Inc.
SUDDENLY, OUT OF NOWHERE, A HAIL OF BULLETS RIPS THE FABRIC OF HIS SOPWITH CAMEL!
WITH UNBELIEVABLE SKILL HE GUIDES THE STRICKEN CRAFT BACK TO THE AERODROME
FEARING A FIERY EXPLOSION, HE LEAPS FROM THE COCKPIT!
WHAT'S A SUPPER DISH DOING ON THE RUNWAY?!
SCHULZ 11-9

WHY DOES YOUR DOG STAND IN THE BACKYARD JUST STARING AT HIS DOGHOUSE?
© 1993 United Feature Syndicate, Inc.
THAT STUPID RED BARON..LOOK WHAT HE DID TO MY PLANE...
SCHULZ 11-10

ON VETERANS DAY I ALWAYS GO OVER TO BILL MAULDIN'S HOUSE TO QUAFF A FEW ROOT BEERS..
BILL KNEW MY HERO, AUDIE MURPHY..
11-11
© 1993 United Feature Syndicate, Inc.
I'VE TOLD BILL HOW I MET CAPTAIN HARRY TRUMAN IN FRANCE...
BUT BILL NEVER BELIEVES ME..

SOMETIMES, I LIE AWAKE AT NIGHT, AND I ASK, "WHY ME?"
11-13
© 1993 United Feature Syndicate, Inc.
THEN A VOICE ANSWERS, "NOTHING PERSONAL.. YOUR NAME JUST HAPPENED TO COME UP.."

PEANUTS®
by
SCHULZ

11-14
© 1993 United Feature Syndicate, Inc.

WHAT HAPPENED TO HIM?
I THINK IT'S HAPPENED BEFORE..
HE GETS HYPNOTIZED WATCHING THE ZAMBONI GO AROUND..
SCHULZ

THIS CAN OF DOG FOOD COST EIGHTY-NINE CENTS..
THIS FROZEN DINNER YOU'RE HAVING TONIGHT COST THREE DOLLARS AND FIFTY CENTS..
11-16
MOM AND DAD SHOULD TRADE YOU IN FOR ANOTHER DOG..
© 1993 United Feature Syndicate, Inc.
STOP GRINNING
SCHULZ

MY DAD'S TAKING ME TO ANOTHER HOCKEY GAME TONIGHT..
11 17
I THINK WE'RE GOING TO SEE THE "MIGHTY FLAMINGOS"
"DUCKS," MARCIE
© 1993 United Feature Syndicate, Inc.
SOMETHING LIKE THAT..
DON'T GET RUN OVER BY THE ZUCCHINI..
ZAMBONI, SIR..
YOU'RE GETTING THERE, MARCIE
SCHULZ

I NEED HELP WITH MY HOMEWORK
WHICH SUBJECT?
11-20
SUBJECT?
© 1993 United Feature Syndicate, Inc.
YOU MEAN WE HAVE SUBJECTS?
SCHULZ

DID YOU KNOW IT TOOK LEO TOLSTOY SIX YEARS TO WRITE "WAR AND PEACE"?
11-19
I KNOW HOW HE MUST HAVE FELT..
© 1993 United Feature Syndicate, Inc.
I'VE BEEN WORKING ON THIS STORY NOW FOR OVER HALF AN HOUR..
SCHULZ

I'VE DECIDED TO SPEND THE REST OF MY LIFE LOOKING FOR "THE BIG ROCK CANDY MOUNTAIN"
11-22
© 1993 United Feature Syndicate, Inc.
I DIDN'T FIND IT TODAY, BUT MAYBE I'LL FIND IT TOMORROW..
IF YOU REALLY WANT SOMETHING IN THIS LIFE, YOU HAVE TO BE DETERMINED!
IF I DON'T FIND IT TOMORROW, I THINK I'LL QUIT LOOKING..
SCHULZ

11-23
HAS THE SCHOOL BUS COME YET?
WHY DON'T YOU OPEN YOUR EYES AND SEE FOR YOURSELF?
© 1993 United Feature Syndicate, Inc.
IT'S TOO EARLY IN THE MORNING TO GO TO ALL THAT TROUBLE..
SCHULZ

YES, MA'AM, I WALKED TO SCHOOL IN THE RAIN..
11-24
© 1993 United Feature Syndicate, Inc.
YES, MA'AM..MY WET HAIR IS DRIPPING ON THE DESK, AND THE WATER SEEMS TO BE RUNNING DOWN THE AISLE...
NO, MA'AM, IT'S THE KIDS BEHIND ME WHO ARE MAKING THE LITTLE PAPER SAILBOATS..
SCHULZ

THIS FOOTBALL LOOKS LIKE A THANKSGIVING TURKEY WITHOUT THE DRUMSTICKS..
CATCH THE TURKEY, SIR! WHITE MEAT OR DARK MEAT? SAVE ME THE WISHBONE!
11-25
THE TURKEY FELL OFF THE TABLE, SIR..
I HATE PLAYING WITH YOU, MARCIE!
© 1993 United Feature Syndicate, Inc.
SCHULZ

SURE, I CAN COUNT.. I SEE EIGHT FINGERS AND TWO THUMBS...
AND ONE NOSE, AND TWO EYES, AND ONE MOUTH, AND TWO EARS...
© 1993 United Feature Syndicate, Inc.
11-26
AND ONE BIG SISTER!

IT'S GOING TO BE COLD TONIGHT SO I THOUGHT YOU MIGHT WANT TO USE THIS BEDROLL..
11-27
© 1993 United Feature Syndicate, Inc.
THOUGHTFUL, BUT SORT OF USELESS..
SCHULZ

I WONDER IF THEY HAVE FRACTIONS IN HEAVEN..
NO FRACTIONS, SIR..NO DECIMALS, EITHER...
HOW ABOUT COMMAS?
© 1993 United Feature Syndicate, Inc.
THERE HAVE TO BE COMMAS, SIR.. WE CAN'T AVOID THEM
11-29
ETERNITY'S GOING TO BE LONGER THAN I THOUGHT..
SCHULZ

CAN YOU SEE THE SCHOOL BUS?
NOT YET
© 1993 United Feature Syndicate, Inc.
I'VE CHANGED MY MIND..I DON'T THINK I'LL GET ON THE BUS..
WHY NOT?
12-1
MY LUNCH JUST WENT HOME..
SCHULZ

HEY, CHUCK, HOW ABOUT A FOOTBALL GAME TOMORROW?
YOU KNOW, A REGULAR STRAIGHT AHEAD, DOWN IN THE DIRT, IN YOUR FACE, ROCK 'EM, SOCK 'EM, ANYTHING GOES, GOOD OLD FASHIONED FOOTBALL GAME!
© 1993 United Feature Syndicate, Inc.
IS THE LIBRARY OPEN TOMORROW?
SCHULZ
12-2

OKAY, CHUCK..HEADS OR TAILS...YOU CALL IT..
12-3
© 1993 United Feature Syndicate, Inc.
TELL YOUR PLAYER TO WAIT 'TIL THE COIN COMES DOWN!
SCHULZ

GET READY, MARCIE.. HERE COMES THE KICKOFF..
I'M READY, SIR..RESEARCH SHOWS THAT IF A GIRL DOES NOT PARTICIPATE IN SPORTS BY THE TIME SHE'S TEN, SHE PROBABLY WON'T WHEN SHE'S THIRTY-FIVE..
© 1993 United Feature Syndicate, Inc.
12-4
BONK!
YOU'LL NEVER BE THIRTY-FIVE, MARCIE..
SCHULZ

OKAY, FRANKLIN, GO STRAIGHT OUT, THEN CUT RIGHT, AND I'LL HIT YOU WITH THE BOMB..
AREN'T YOU ON THE OTHER TEAM, SWEETIE?
MY GLASSES ARE WET..I CAN'T SEE A THING..
SCHULZ
12-6
© 1993 United Feature Syndicate, Inc.

WHERE AM I?
WHO'S GOT THE BALL?
SOMEBODY CALL THE VET!
IS IT STILL RAINING OR AM I BLEEDING?
ISN'T THIS GREAT, CHUCK? GOOD OLD FASHIONED, DOWN IN THE DIRT FOOTBALL!
12-7 © 1993 United Feature Syndicate, Inc.
SCHULZ

© 1993 United Feature Syndicate, Inc.
12-8
WE'RE NOT LETTING A LITTLE RAIN SPOIL OUR FUN, ARE WE, CHUCK?
DID SHE SAY "RAIN" OR "PAIN"?
SCHULZ

© 1993 United Feature Syndicate, Inc.
THANKS FOR THE GAME, CHUCK! I HAD LOTS OF FUN..YOU GUYS HAD FUN, TOO, DIDN'T YOU?
LOTS OF FUN..
FROM NOW ON I'M GOING TO BE A HOUSE DOG..
SCHULZ
12-9

BOY, AFTER A GAME LIKE THAT IT'D BE NICE TO SIT IN A HOT TUB..
I'LL SAY IT WOULD..
12-10
© 1993 United Feature Syndicate, Inc.
A LOT BETTER THAN A COLD WATER DISH
SCHULZ

WASN'T THAT FUN, MARCIE? GOOD OLD FASHIONED, PLAY IN THE RAIN, DOWN IN THE DIRT, FOOTBALL!
I THINK I LOST MY SHOES..
12-11
© 1993 United Feature Syndicate, Inc.
AND NOW IT'S STARTING TO SNOW! WE SHOULD PLAY AGAIN TOMORROW..
I NEVER KNEW LIFE COULD BE SO BEAUTIFUL!
SCHULZ

IF YOU'RE COLLECTING FOR CHARITY, WHAT CHARITY ARE YOU COLLECTING FOR?
© 1993 United Feature Syndicate, Inc.
12-13
SCHULZ

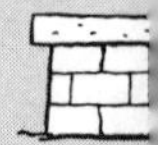

12-14
I HAVE TO READ A BOOK DURING CHRISTMAS VACATION..
TRY THIS ONE.. IT'S A REAL PAGE-TURNER
© 1993 United Feature Syndicate, Inc.
I HATE TURNING PAGES
SCHULZ

THIS IS THE BOOK I HAVE TO READ FOR SCHOOL..I WANT YOU TO READ IT FOR ME..
12-15
YOU MEAN I'M SUPPOSED TO READ IT WHILE YOU JUST SIT HERE AND LISTEN..
© 1993 United Feature Syndicate, Inc.
LISTEN ?
SCHULZ

PEANUTS®
by
SCHULZ

12-5 © 1993 United Feature Syndicate, Inc.
..SO WHAT WE'RE TALKING ABOUT HERE IS EMPOWERMENT THROUGH INNER DIALOGUE HOPEFULLY LEADING TO LIFE ENHANCEMENT..
SCHULZ

ALL RIGHT, I READ YOUR BOOK FOR YOU... NOW, WHAT DO I DO?
NOW, YOU WRITE THE REPORT..
I HOPE YOU APPRECIATE ALL THIS..
© 1993 United Feature Syndicate, Inc.
12-16
I'LL SEND YOU A CHRISTMAS CARD
SCHULZ

ALL RIGHT, I WROTE YOUR BOOK REPORT FOR YOU.. SEE WHAT YOU THINK..
"THIS WAS THE MOST EXCITING BOOK I HAVE EVER READ..I LIKED ALL THE CHARACTERS"
© 1993 United Feature Syndicate, Inc.
12/17
"THE DESCRIPTIONS WERE BEAUTIFUL, AND THE STORY VERY SUSPENSEFUL"
I DON'T KNOW..IF I HAD READ IT, I WOULDN'T HAVE LIKED IT THAT MUCH
SCHULZ

BEND DOWN..
12-18 © 1993 United Feature Syndicate, Inc.
SCHULZ

ONE OF THE GREAT JOYS IN LIFE IS SLIDING ON AN ICY SIDEWALK..
12-20
© 1993 United Feature Syndicate, Inc.
JOE 'ICE FOLLIES'..
SCHULZ

YES, MA'AM..IT'S COLD OUTSIDE...
12-21
I'D LIKE AN ICE CREAM CONE, PLEASE
DO YOU MIND MITTEN MONEY? THIS IS SOME MONEY THAT'S BEEN IN MY MITTEN SINCE LAST WINTER..
ONE MORE QUESTION..
© 1993 United Feature Syndicate, Inc.
HOW DO YOU EAT ICE CREAM THROUGH A WOOLEN SCARF?
SCHULZ

WHERE'S MY BIG FURRY HAT?
HAS ANYONE SEEN MY BIG FURRY HAT?
12-22
© 1993 United Feature Syndicate, Inc.
SCHULZ

12-23
I THINK I'VE LEARNED SOMETHING
YOU CAN SLIDE DOWN THE STEPS..
© 1993 United Feature Syndicate, Inc.
BUT YOU CAN'T SLIDE..
UP THE STEPS..
SCHULZ

© 1993 United Feature Syndicate, Inc.
SCHULZ
MERRY CHRISTMAS
12-24

Dear Mom and Dad,
Thank you for the wonderful present. It is something I have always wanted.
12-25
© 1993 United Feature Syndicate, Inc.
SCHULZ

WOULD YOU BE OFFENDED IF I EXCHANGED THE PRESENT YOU GAVE ME FOR CHRISTMAS?
12-27
I DIDN'T GIVE YOU A PRESENT FOR CHRISTMAS..
© 1993 United Feature Syndicate, Inc.
AND DON'T THINK I DIDN'T NOTICE!
SCHULZ

The Dog-That Most Magnificent of All Creatures.
12-28
WHAT KIND OF DOG ARE YOU TALKING ABOUT?
© 1993 United Feature Syndicate, Inc.
Any Dog
SCHULZ

I'VE ALWAYS WONDERED HOW THE ZAMBONI GOT OFF THE ICE..
© 1993 United Feature Syndicate, Inc.
12-29
SCHULZ

" DR. MORTIMER'S VOICE SANK ALMOST TO A WHISPER, AND HE SAID, 'MR. HOLMES, THEY WERE THE FOOTPRINTS OF A GIGANTIC HOUND!' "
WELL, THAT'S ENOUGH READING FOR TONIGHT..
© 1993 United Feature Syndicate, Inc.
12/30
AND I NEVER SLEEP AGAIN FOR THE REST OF MY LIFE..
SCHULZ

SHALL WE READ SOME MORE OF "THE HOUND OF THE BASKERVILLES" TONIGHT ?
12-31
© 1993 United Feature Syndicate, Inc.
OKAY, I'M READY..
SCHULZ